Captain Brabant took a step towards her and Caroline backed away instinctively. One brow arched in ironic amusement as he saw her withdraw. 'My dear Miss Whiston, pray do not be alarmed! You have nothing to fear from me. But—a companion! How very inappropriate!'

'I do not know how you could be the judge of such matters, sir!' Caroline snapped, forgetting that he was to all intents and purposes her host, and giving in to her indignation. 'Upon my word, you have a strange concept of appropriate behaviour! What is appropriate about accosting respectable ladies as they take a walk in the woods? I believe that you have been away at sea so long that you forget your manners!'

She saw him grin. It seemed an unacceptable response to her annoyance.

'Maybe that accounts for it,' he murmured. 'Deprived of the improving company of the fair sex… Indeed, ma'am, I think you must be right!'

A young woman disappears.
A husband is suspected of murder.
Stirring times for all the neighbourhood in

The STEEPWOOD
Scandal

Book 4

When the debauched Marquis of Sywell won
Steepwood Abbey years ago at cards, it led to the death
of the then Earl of Yardley. Now he's caused scandal
again by marrying a girl out of his class—and young
enough to be his granddaughter! After being married
only a short time, the Marchioness has disappeared,
leaving no trace of her whereabouts. There is every
expectation that yet more scandals will emerge, though
no one yet knows just how shocking they will be.

The four villages surrounding the Steepwood Abbey
estate are in turmoil, not only with the dire goings-on
at the Abbey, but also with their own affairs. Each
story in **The Steepwood Scandal** follows the mystery
behind the disappearance of the young woman, and the
individual romances of lovers connected in some way
with the intrigue.

**Regency Drama
intrigue, mischief...and marriage**

A COMPANION OF QUALITY

Nicola Cornick

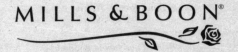

MILLS & BOON®

All the characters in this book have no existence outside the imagination of the author, and have no relation whatsoever to anyone bearing the same name or names. They are not even distantly inspired by any individual known or unknown to the author, and all the incidents are pure invention.

*First published in Great Britain 2001
Harlequin Mills & Boon Limited,
Eton House, 18-24 Paradise Road, Richmond, Surrey TW9 1SR*

© Harlequin Books S.A. 2001

Special thanks and acknowledgment are given to Nicola Cornick
for her contribution to The Steepwood Scandal series

ISBN 0 263 82845 X

*Set in Times Roman 10½ on 12½ pt.
119-0801-59864*

*Printed and bound in Spain
by Litografia Rosés S.A., Barcelona*

Nicola Cornick is passionate about many things: her country cottage and its garden, her two small cats, her husband and her writing. Though not necessarily in that order! She has always been fascinated by history, both as her chosen subject at university and subsequently as an engrossing hobby. She works as a university administrator and finds her writing the perfect antidote to the demands of life in a busy office.

Nicola Cornick's second novel in **The Steepwood Scandal**, *An Unlikely Suitor*, follows Lewis's sister Lavender's story. Coming soon.

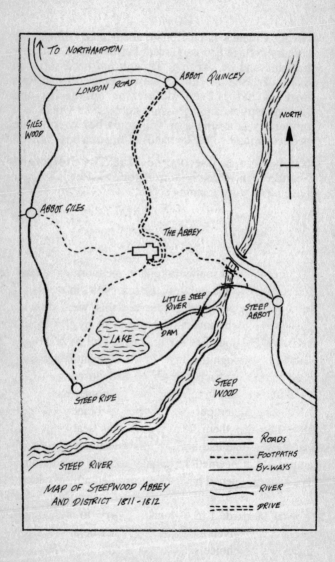

TO NORTHAMPTON

LONDON ROAD

ABBOT QUINCEY

GILES WOOD

NORTH

ABBOT GILES

THE ABBEY

LITTLE STEEP RIVER

STEEP ABBOT

DAM

LAKE

STEEP WOOD

STEEP RIDE

STEEP RIVER

MAP OF STEEPWOOD ABBEY
AND DISTRICT 1811 - 1812

ROADS
FOOTPATHS
BY-WAYS
RIVER
DRIVE

Chapter One

November, 1811

The room faced south-east and in the morning it was full of sun and the light off the sea. Now, in the dark of a November evening, the curtains were drawn against the night and the room was lit by lamp and firelight. The sound of the sea could still be heard, a faint echo through the dark. Lewis Brabant rested his head against the back of his chair and closed his eyes.

'So you're not in any hurry to go home, then.'

Richard Slater put two glasses of brandy on the table between them and resumed his seat opposite Lewis. His tone had been mildly questioning and for a moment it seemed he would receive no answer. Then Lewis opened his eyes and smiled a little reluctantly.

'No, Richard. I'm damnably sorry to be going home at all! Given a choice, I'd rather be at sea. But there was no choice…'

'That holds true for both of us—for different reasons,' his friend said, the tiniest shade of bitterness in his voice as he cast one rueful glance down at the injured leg that still caused him to limp a little. He picked up the brandy glass and held it up in an ironic toast.

'To the landlocked!'

They clinked glasses. 'You have done your prison out well,' Lewis observed, his keen blue gaze travelling around the study approvingly. The walls were panelled like the wardroom of a ship, a brass sextant shone on the table by the window, and over by the bookcases was a fine telescope in a battered leather case.

'At least I still have the smell and sound of the sea,' Richard commented, 'unlike you! Northamptonshire's a dashed odd place for an Admiral to retire! What made your father choose the county in the first place?'

Lewis shrugged. 'My mother had family connections in the area and indeed, they seemed happy enough there.' He took a mouthful of brandy and paused to savour the taste. 'This is very fine, Richard! French, isn't it? Was it smuggled in for you?'

Richard grinned. 'Devil a bit! A favour from a friend.'

'I know what you mean.' Lewis stretched. 'Never fear, I won't outstay my welcome here, despite the excellence of the brandy! You and your sister have been most hospitable, but I'm for London tomorrow

and from there it's but a day's drive to Hewly.' He
grimaced. 'I suppose I must call it home now.'

'Fanny will be sorry to see you go so soon,'
Richard murmured, 'as will I. If you feel the need to
see the sea again—'

'I'll be working too hard on the estate to spare any
thought for my past life!' Lewis ran a hand through
his thick, fair hair. He gave his friend a rueful grin.
'But perhaps you will both visit me? It would be good
to see old friends…'

'Delighted, old chap!' Richard shot him a quizzical
look. 'Not looking forward to life amidst a parcel of
women?'

Lewis put his empty glass down gently on the table
between them. 'Not a flattering description, Richard,
but I take your point! M'sister writes that not only is
she joined by our cousin Julia, but now there's some
spinsterish companion to do the knitting and fuss over
the flowers! Of all the things I need—some Friday-
faced female at the dinner-table!'

'Mrs Chessford could hardly be described in such
terms,' Richard said slyly. 'You must be eager to see
her again!'

Lewis gave his friend a hard stare. 'Julia's always
welcome at Hewly, I suppose, though I would deem
it a little slow for her tastes!'

Richard nodded. His sister had been in London during the previous season and had returned with plenty
of gossip about the dashing widow Julia Chessford.
It seemed unlikely, however, that Lewis would appreciate a rehearsal of Mrs Chessford's amours. There

had been a time, Richard knew, when Lewis was more than a little smitten with Julia himself.

'How long is it since you were there?' he asked neutrally, steering the conversation away from areas that were clearly not for discussion.

Lewis sighed. 'It was in '05, just after Trafalgar. Father's health had already started to decline then, but it was a slow process. It is only since his recent attack that he has been bedridden and incapable of directing his affairs.'

'Does he show any sign of improvement?' Richard limped over to retrieve the brandy decanter and refill their glasses.

Lewis shook his head slowly. 'Lavender writes that he is occasionally well enough to sit downstairs, but he recognises no one and speaks not at all. It's a damnable shame for so active a man.'

'Isn't Hewly close to Steepwood Abbey?' Richard asked. He leant down to stoke the fire. 'Dashed rum place, as I recall. My Uncle Rodney was a crony of Sywell and Cleeve years ago, before he forswore the drink and the gaming tables! The tales he told!'

Lewis laughed. 'I don't believe that Sywell has ever forsaken the drink and the cards—nor the women! Yes, Hewly is close by the Abbey, but I've never met the Marquis. By all accounts he continues to scandalise the neighbourhood. M'sister wrote that he had married his bailiff's ward less than a year past!'

Richard looked amused. 'Perhaps Cupid's dart will

strike you too, Lewis! Just the thing to help you settle down and rusticate!'

Lewis raised one eyebrow in a disbelieving grimace. 'I thank you, but I do not look to take a wife! Not until I find a woman who can match my last ship!'

'The *Dauntless*?' Richard laughed. 'What were her qualities then, old fellow? I thought she was a leaky old tub that no one else would dare put to sea in!'

'Nonsense!' Lewis grinned mockingly. 'She was a beautiful ship! She was elegant and courageous and she would risk all to gain all!' His smile faded. 'And until I find a woman to rival her, Richard, I shall stay single!'

Miss Caroline Whiston put her leather-bound book of Shakespearean sonnets to one side with a sigh. No one had ever compared her to a summer's day, and if they had she would probably have boxed their ears, knowing their intentions could not be honourable. She knew of too many governesses who had made the mistake of believing in romance and had lived to regret it. Even so it would have been pleasant for once—just once—to meet a man who was neither a rake nor a worthy.

Ever since she had become a governess companion some ten years previously, Caroline had secretly classified all the men that she met into these two groups. The rakes predominated. They could be the fathers, brothers, relatives and friends of her youthful charges and they generally considered themselves irresistible, believing that Caroline should feel the same way. These she dealt with using a mixture of severity and hauteur, resorting very occasionally to physical violence to deter their advances. None of them ever persisted. Caroline was not pretty enough to make it worth their while, and she made sure that she concealed rather than accentuated those features that did give her distinction. Her beautiful chestnut hair was ruthlessly drawn back and confined into a bun. She wore drab, shapeless clothing. Her manner instilled respect into both her pupils and their parents alike.

'I say,' the elder brother of her previous charges had complained with feeling, 'Miss Whiston has a dashed cutting way with her! I'd sooner kiss a snake than try for some sport there!'

Then there were the worthies. These were not as dangerous as the rakes but had to be deterred all the same. They might include a tutor or curate who would imagine that Caroline would make a suitable helpmeet. To these she was kind but firm. She had no intention of exchanging the drudgery of an upper servant for that of unpaid maid of all work in a vicarage, not even for the respectability of a wedding ring.

Caroline sighed again. She was growing cold, for the November mornings had turned frosty recently and not even the thickness of her winter cloak was proof against the chill that seeped up through her boots and was currently spreading through all her limbs. Her scarlet velvet dress, a most impractical present from the kind-hearted mother of one of her charges, was more for show than warmth. Caroline knew it was an affectation to wear an evening gown when she was out walking in the forest in the dawn, but after all, there was no one to see and it was the only time she could indulge in a little luxury. Still, she should be getting back. She shivered. It was cold, and she would be late, and then Julia would be as sharp and scratchy as only she could be.

Caroline tucked the book into her pocket, picked up her basket and started to pick her way through the undergrowth towards the path. The frosty twigs crunched under her boots. Spiders' webs whitened with ice shone like spun silver in the sun. It was very quiet. These early mornings were the only solitude that Caroline could find at present, for she was at Julia Chessford's beck and call all day long and even at night, if Mrs Chessford were suddenly struck down with insomnia. Caroline, who had at first interpreted Julia's invitation to stay at Hewly as a request from a friend, had been quick to realise that she was in fact nothing more than a servant. The days when the two of them had been schoolgirls together were long gone.

Then there was Admiral Brabant, who required constant nursing and whose illness cast a shadow like a pall over Hewly Manor. His latest attack had occurred some three months previously, before Caroline had come to Hewly, and had left him incapable of running the estate any longer. The servants whispered that the Admiral would not outlast the winter snows and their gloomy predictions added to the general air of misery. Hewly Manor was not a cheerful place.

Life for Caroline might have been very different.

She and Julia Chessford had studied together not fif-
teen minutes' walk away, at the Guarding Academy
in Steep Abbot. In those days, Julia had been Admiral
Brabant's god-daughter and ward, and Caroline had
been the daughter of a baronet. A spendthrift baronet,
as it had turned out. Caroline could only be grateful
that he had staved off his ruin until she was old
enough to earn her own living. He had died when she
was seventeen, the title had devolved on a distant
cousin, and the estate had had to be sold to pay his
debts.

Caroline stepped out of the trees and on to the path,
and almost immediately heard the sound of horse's
hooves striking against the frosty earth. Whoever was
approaching was riding quickly. It sounded like a single horseman coming from the west rather than from
the Northampton road to the east. Caroline hesitated.
She had no wish to be found alone and loitering in
the middle of the wood, and fortunately there was a
woodcutter's tumbledown hut set a little way back
from the track. She hurried to take cover there. She
did not fear poachers or highwaymen—that would
have been foolish imagination—but there was no
sense in courting danger by making herself obvious.

As the horseman came around the corner of the
path he slowed his mount to a walk, affording
Caroline the chance to get a good look at him. She
peeked through the broken doorway of the hut and
heaved a silent sigh of relief. Here was no rake, she
was sure. He looked far more like a worthy, with his
fair, fine-drawn looks and air of abstraction. He was

neatly but plainly attired in a black coat and buff breeches, and his boots were scuffed from hard riding. No London rake, then, but a sober country gentleman. Medium height, medium build, altogether unremarkable. Perhaps he was a poet enjoying the morning air just as she had been. Caroline kept quite still and waited for him to pass by.

It seemed, however, that the gentleman was in no hurry. She watched as he sprang down from the saddle and pulled the horse's reins over its head. It was a fine animal, a high-stepping grey with intelligent eyes, and she saw the man stroke its nose and speak quietly to it as he led it along the path towards her. The horse was limping a little and had obviously gone lame. Caroline held her breath and hoped that its rider would not decide to stop for a rest.

It was the mouse that was her undoing. She considered herself an indomitable female, but ever since Julia had put a dead mouse in her bed at school, Caroline had had a fear of tiny furry mammals. This one ran across her foot and she made an involuntary movement, sending the dead leaves swirling through the doorway of the hut and frightening a pheasant that was scratching around outside. The bird flew off giving its harsh cry and the horse, no doubt still unsettled by the incident that had turned it lame, reared up and almost knocked the gentleman to the ground.

Caroline drew back hastily into the shadows but she knew she was too late. Her abrupt movement had revealed a flash of scarlet velvet and it was useless to just stand there pretending that she was invisible. As she hesitated, the gentleman regained his balance and turned sharply towards the hut. For a long moment he stared straight at her, then he dropped the horse's reins and took a step towards her.

Caroline's heart was racing suddenly. She knew that the sensible course of action would be to step forward and apologise, but even as she thought this, she was turning to scramble through a gap in the back wall and stumble down amongst the leaves and brambles on the other side.

Her legs were shaking as she tried to steady herself and tear her cloak from the grip of the rough masonry that snagged at the material. She heard the scrape of loose stone behind her and was filled with a heady panic. Surely he was not following her! He had looked so harmless, so very worthy…

It was at that moment that Caroline discovered the extent of her mistake. A hand caught hold of her wrist and pulled her round to face him with a force that almost knocked the breath from her body. The hood of her cloak fell back and her hair tumbled all about her shoulders. She grasped instinctively at his arm for support, and felt the hard muscle beneath her fingers, the indisputable evidence of a man in excellent physical condition. So much for her thoughts of a dreamy poet with more interest in pursuits of the intellect than those of the body! Caroline raised her gaze to his face and discovered that the far-seeing eyes that she had imagined were dwelling on some piece of verse were a hard blue, cold as a stormy sea. For a long moment they stared at each other, and then Caroline saw a hint of laughter lighten his face and for some reason she felt her legs tremble again.

'Well…' There was lazy amusement in the man's voice. 'Not the poacher I'd expected, but I cannot find it in me to be sorry! Hold still, sweetheart—' He had felt her struggle and held on to her with insulting ease. 'You owe me something at least for frightening my horse!'

Not a worthy but a rake, Caroline found herself thinking, as she felt him shift his grip a little so that he could pull her into his arms. This had to be the first time that she had made such an error of judgement, and she was not the only one.

'You are making a mistake—' Her words were lost as she found herself being thoroughly kissed. The roughness of his cheek brushed hers; he smelled of leather and fresh air and lemon cologne. It was delicious and she was utterly shocked with herself for even thinking so.

'You were saying?'

The gentleman had let her go sufficiently to look down into her face. Caroline saw his eyes sweep appreciatively over her chestnut curls and linger on the red evening gown. And no wonder. It was cut low and she could feel the sting of the cold air against her bare skin. Drawing her cloak closely about her, Caroline glared at him.

'I was trying to tell you that you were making a mistake…' The words came out with considerably less than her usual authoritative ring. She cleared her throat and frowned slightly. He was watching her with the same lazy mockery that she had heard in his voice and it distracted her.

'What I mean is… You should not… I am not—'

'I would hate you to think that I had kissed you by mistake, ma'am,' the gentleman said politely, and it seemed to Caroline that he was wilfully misunderstanding her. 'I cannot possibly let you go under such a misapprehension. Allow me…'

Caroline gave a little squeak of dismay as he pulled her close again. This was a deeper kiss. Her lips parted under the skilful pressure of his. He tasted cold. Sensation swept through Caroline and left her shivering. She could not believe what was happening to her and could not begin to understand *why* she was letting it happen. With a supreme effort of will she tried to free herself again, and he let her go immediately.

'Listen to me.' She put a hand out as though to ward him off, although he had made no further move towards her. 'I am trying to explain to you that you are making a serious error, sir! I am not what you think me, and you, sir—' She broke off, unusually lost for words as she considered his face.

She had been wrong to think his looks fine-drawn. On a woman, the high cheekbones and chiselled features might have appeared delicate, but there was too much authority and determination in his face to give any hint of weakness. Those blue eyes held a disconcerting look of appraisal and the thick fair hair that Caroline had wanted to touch… She cleared her throat self-consciously, aware that he was still watching her.

'I believe that you must be Captain Brabant,' she said, with as much composure as she could muster. 'I am Caroline Whiston. I am staying at the Manor.'

A frown had come into the gentleman's eyes, replacing the look of appreciative amusement that had lingered there. This time when his gaze considered her it held no warmth. Caroline drew herself up a little. She dared not think what she looked like, her hair all tousled and her lips rosy from his kisses.

'I beg your pardon, ma'am,' he said slowly, 'but are we acquainted? Or do you include clairvoyance in your gifts, that you already know my name?'

It was on the tip of Caroline's tongue to say that she felt he had treated her as rather more than an acquaintance already, but she knew that there was no point in provoking further trouble. There was no doubt that this could only be Lewis Brabant and she cursed herself that she had not recognised him from the start. His resemblance to his sister was sufficiently strong that she should have guessed his identity straight away, rather than realising only when he was at close quarters. Very close quarters, she amended. And now she was well and truly in the suds, since this man was heir to Hewly Manor and, more to the point, Julia's former fiancé...

She realised that Captain Brabant was still awaiting her response and dropped a slight curtsey.

'No, sir, we have not met,' she said, with tolerable composure, 'but you have a great look of your sister about you so it is small wonder that I recognised you. The household has been expecting you home this se'ennight and more.'

'I see,' Captain Brabant said, and Caroline had the disconcerting feeling that he saw more than was comfortable. She reflected ruefully that she felt much as the cabin boy must have done when Captain Brabant was inspecting his crew on the quarterdeck. Those blue eyes were disturbingly perceptive.

'Forgive me, Miss Whiston,' he said, 'but when you said that you were a guest at the Manor—'

Caroline felt a blush rising. 'You misunderstand me, sir,' she said hastily. 'I am not a guest of your father's but companion to your cousin…to Mrs Chessford.'

'Julia's companion? You?' Captain Brabant took a step towards her and Caroline backed away from him instinctively. One brow arched in ironic amusement as he saw her withdraw. 'My dear Miss Whiston, pray do not be alarmed! You have nothing to fear from me! But—a companion! How very inappropriate!'

'I do not know how you could be a judge of such matters, sir!' Caroline snapped, forgetting that he was to all intents and purposes her host, and giving in to her indignation. 'Upon my word, you have a strange concept of appropriate behaviour! What is appropriate about accosting respectable ladies as they take a walk in the woods? I believe that you must have been away at sea so long that you forget your manners!'

She saw him grin. It seemed an unacceptable response to her annoyance.

'Maybe that accounts for it,' he murmured. 'Deprived of the improving company of the fair sex… Indeed, ma'am, I think you must be right!'

'Fustian, sir!' Caroline retorted, the colour flaring in her face. 'I do not believe that you have been deprived of female companionship! Such freedom of manner argues that the reverse is true—' She broke off, realising that this exasperating man had driven her to express views that should have remained private. Severe Miss Whiston never normally allowed herself a vulgar display of opinion. It was not at all proper for a governess companion.

She bit back her words, trying to ignore the Captain's infuriating smile. 'Well, that is nothing to the purpose!' she finished sharply. 'Good day, sir! I shall leave you to complete your journey alone.'

'That seems rather pointless when we are both travelling in the same direction,' the Captain said politely. 'Permit me to escort you back, Miss Whiston! We may become better acquainted!'

Caroline gritted her teeth. That was the last thing she wanted, and if Julia should witness Captain Brabant's arrival at the Manor with her in attendance… Well, it did not really bear thinking about.

'No, indeed—'

'Perhaps you could explain why you were running away from me,' the Captain continued affably, as though she had not spoken. 'After all, it was your own behaviour that sparked the whole incident!'

Caroline blushed. She knew that he was right, but felt it was not gallant of him to remind her. 'I apologise, sir,' she said tightly. 'I fear I was nervous. You must think it quite odd in me—'

'I do! To startle my horse and then to run off as though you were a miscreant! What was I to do?'

'You cannot truly have thought me a poacher, sir—' Caroline stopped, realising that she was once again being drawn into a ridiculous conversation.

'Not once I had caught you, of course,' Captain Brabant said, with a quirk of his brows. 'When I was holding you, I thought—'

'Thank you, sir, it is best forgotten, I think!'

The Captain seemed undiscouraged. 'This must be yours, I think, ma'am.' He was holding out her book of sonnets to her. 'Shakespeare? Do you also read the romantic poets?'

Caroline practically snatched the book from his hand, thrusting it back into her pocket. Why must the man insist on making conversation?

'I have little time,' she said crossly.

'For poetry or for romance?' Once again he was smiling at her quizzically.

Caroline concentrated on picking her way through the brambles and did not reply.

'You would probably find walking more comfortable in suitable clothing,' the Captain continued, from close behind her. 'That evening dress, whilst most appealing, is not very practical. Though with the boots,' he sounded as though he was giving the matter real consideration, 'it is particularly fetching—'

Caroline set her lips in a tight line and still said nothing. She could not believe how unfortunately everything was falling out. Here was Captain Brabant, authoritative, assured and utterly unlike Julia had described him. Why could he not have been the gentle dreamer of Julia's memory, or at the least a bluff old sea-dog with hair prematurely grey and an everlasting fund of boring tales? She watched him covertly as he retrieved his horse from the forest edge, where it had been happily munching its way through a brambly hedge. She was forced to acknowledge that there was something powerfully attractive about Captain Brabant's loose-limbed grace, something deceptive about that air of abstraction. A thinker as well as a man of action. In Caroline's experience that made him all the more dangerous.

It was the worst possible luck that they were obliged to be under the same roof, but she comforted herself with the thought that she need not see him much. Now that he knew she was not a guest but a servant his interest must surely wane, and any further *unsuitable* interest would have to be discouraged. It was a pity that he did not have enough proper feeling himself to understand the indelicacy of their circumstances. She was sure that she could hear him whistling under his breath, a sure sign that he did not take the situation seriously.

'Your basket, Miss Whiston.'

Caroline jumped. Captain Brabant gave her a slight bow and presented her with the woven reed basket, a few solitary mushrooms rolling around in its base. She had dropped it when she ran away, and she could see the rest of her crop scattered about on the path and in the undergrowth. He followed her gaze.

'We could pick them all up, I suppose,' he mused, 'although in a ballgown it would be quite difficult—'

'Pray do not put yourself to any trouble, Captain!' Caroline said hastily, feeling cross and foolish in equal measure. Would the man never cease to remind her of her idiocy in wandering about in the scarlet dress? Now she was well served for her vanity! The dress would be banished to the back of the wardrobe and never see the light of day again!

She reluctantly allowed Captain Brabant to fall into step beside her as they made their way along the path towards Steep Abbot. Caroline tried to preserve a chilly silence, but found that that seemed to make her even more aware of the Captain's presence at her side. Eventually she was forced into speech by her own self-consciousness.

'Did you have a good journey home, Captain?' she asked politely, picking on the most innocuous topic she could think of. Lewis Brabant smiled at her. It was decidedly unsettling.

'Yes, I thank you. I spent a few nights in London on my way up from Portsmouth. It was strange to be back.'

'Cold as well, I shouldn't wonder,' Caroline said encouragingly, glad to see that he was capable of holding a proper conversation. 'After the Mediterranean, autumn in England must seem very cold.'

There was now a decided twinkle in the Captain's eye. 'Oh, decidedly, ma'am! Cold and wet.'

'It has not rained here for several weeks, although the summer was very wet,' Caroline observed, ignoring the fact that he was now grinning. She knew he was funning her but she was determined to disregard it. She knew how to behave even if he did not.

'I had also forgotten,' the Captain said conversationally, 'how the English are obsessed with the weather! Or perhaps,' he turned slightly to look at her face, 'it is a defence against too personal a conversation? One thing I have *not* forgotten is society's ability to discuss trivia for hours!'

Caroline knew what he meant and she agreed with him. She had spent many a long hour in various drawing-rooms, listening to ladies chatter inconsequentially about something and nothing, gossiping on fortune, connections and scandal. It was galling to think that she was sounding just as hen-witted as they. Yet how to avoid it? She already suspected that Captain Brabant was a man who had little time for prevarication and she felt she had to keep him at arm's length.

She put up the hood of her cloak. The morning was chilly, though the sun was now breaking through the branches. She knew she looked most disheveled, with her hair in disarray, and she was anxious not to arrive at the Manor looking as though she had been dragged through a hedge—or thoroughly kissed.

'Ah,' she heard the smile in Captain Brabant's voice, 'there are other defences, are there not, Miss

Whiston? Hiding away inside your cloak must be one
of them! So I suppose that it is out of the question to
ask you to tell me a little about yourself? After all,
we shall be sharing a roof…'

Caroline did not like the sound of that. The implied
intimacy made her blush and she was glad of the con-
cealment of the hood. They had reached the edge of
the wood now, and Lewis held the gate for her before
leading the horse through. The path crossed the Steep
River and approached the village. The river ran in
lazy bends here, bounded by trees that in the summer
bent down towards the slow, brown waters. This
morning, with the sun gilding the frosty branches and
glittering on the water, it looked very pretty.

'There is little to tell,' Caroline said, coolly. 'I am
a very dull subject. I have been a governess for eleven
years, since I left the Guarding Academy, and I am
now Mrs Chessford's companion. A paid companion,'
she added, to make her meaning crystal clear. For a
long moment, blue eyes met blue, then Lewis Brabant
nodded slightly.

'No one is ever as dull as they pretend, Miss
Whiston! A lady's companion who walks in the forest
wearing a ballgown and reading Shakespeare seems
extraordinary rather than ordinary to me!'

Caroline could feel her colour rising again. 'Nevertheless… I wish you will not pursue it, sir!'

'As you wish…' Caroline could feel him watching
her. 'I did not realise that you were a schoolfriend of
Julia's,' he added thoughtfully. 'I do not remember…'

'That is hardly surprising,' Caroline said sharply.

In her experience, the relatives of her old school-friends, particularly the male ones, had no recollection of her at all. How could they, when she paled into invisibility beside Julia's golden beauty?

Captain Brabant raised his hand in a gesture of surrender. 'Very well, Miss Whiston, we will change the subject, since you evidently think it unsuitable! You are the paid companion here—scarce better than a servant!' His tone had taken on a sarcastic edge. 'Far be it from me to overstep the social distinctions that clearly form the boundaries of your life!'

They had passed the Guarding Academy now and had turned down the cobbled lane that led to the Manor, walking at least four feet apart. Caroline clenched her fists in her pockets. She told herself that she had wanted Captain Brabant to observe the proprieties and it was therefore contrary to feel ill-used when he did precisely that.

They approached the gate of the Manor in silence and Caroline's heart sank to see the Captain's frown deepen as his gaze fell on his inheritance. The five-bar gate was rotten and a couple of the spars had broken off. The wall had long ago tumbled into the road and the drive beyond was overgrown with weeds and grasses. It was almost impossible to distinguish the formal gardens from the orchards, for all was a wilderness.

'Much has changed, has it not?' Lewis Brabant said under his breath, and Caroline felt his gaze linger on her as though she were part of a new, unwelcome order. It was not a pleasant feeling.

The clock on the stables read ten thirty, and somewhere in the house Caroline heard the echo of chimes. She winced. Julia might well be awake by now and wanting help with her toilette. She turned to Lewis Brabant, whose face was set in tense lines as he surveyed his home.

'I will go and tell them that you are here, sir. Excuse me—'

She pushed at the wicket gate leading into the gardens, slipping on the damp moss underfoot in her haste to get inside. Immediately the Captain's arm was about her waist, steadying her and holding her close.

'For all your objections, fate seems determined to throw us together, Miss Whiston,' he murmured in her ear.

'The stables are that way, sir,' Caroline said crossly, trying to free herself. He did not remove his arm and she was obliged to push hard against his chest to make him let her go. She heard him laugh.

'I know it. I was brought up here, if you recall—' He broke off and straightened up suddenly, his arms falling away from her. Caroline spun round. One of the upstairs windows of the Manor was open and a figure was leaning out. Her hair was like spun gold on the breeze. She looked like the princess in a fairy story. Caroline bit her lip.

'Lewis!' the vision called out. 'You are home!'

'Julia!'

Caroline heard Lewis Brabant say the name softly and felt a strange pang of envy. She watched with rueful disbelief as he dropped the reins, pushed the gate open and strode towards the main door. Caroline turned away abruptly, took hold of the horse's bridle and led the grey down the lane towards the stables.

'So that is why Julia has been betrothed three times, married and widowed all in the space that I have been governess and companion to three families!' she whispered in the horse's silky ear. 'Alas that I could study for years and never achieve such a result!'

The horse whickered softly and shook his head, as though in agreement. Caroline sighed as she handed him over to the groom, instructing the lad to take a look at the injured leg. That was that, then. It seemed that Julia would have little difficulty in engaging Captain Brabant's affections once again. Perhaps Lewis had never really forgotten her, despite all that had happened since the two of them had last met. As for his behaviour in the wood, it only served to show him to be a man who trifled with the feelings of others and could not be trusted. Caroline thrust her hands into the pockets of the cloak and reflected that the Captain would receive a dusty answer were he to try such shabby tricks on her again.

Chapter Two

'Pray be careful with those curling tongs, Caroline!' Julia Chessford said fretfully, moving her head to one side to admire the fall of golden ringlets about her shoulders. 'I declare, you are as ham-fisted as a scullery-maid!'

Caroline resisted an immediate urge to press the hot tongs against Julia's ear. 'I fear I am no turn at these matters, not being a trained ladies' maid,' she said evenly. 'It is unfortunate that you gave Letty the evening off—'

'Oh, the worst chance imaginable!' Julia agreed, smiling as she considered her reflection in the mirror. 'But how was I to know that Lewis would choose this of all days to return home? Such bad luck quite oversets one's plans, but we must make shift as best we can! Do hurry, Caroline! We are to dine in ten minutes!'

Caroline moved across to the closet to fetch Julia's wrap, watching as her former friend stood up and turned around slowly to consider her appearance.

There was no denying that Julia looked very beauti-ful. She had huge blue eyes that gave a misleading impression of sweetness and innocence, and the thick golden hair curled lusciously about her rounded face. Her lips were a perfect bow shape, her nose small and straight. Caroline, blessed with a set of features that were less regular, tried to repress her envy. She would not have exchanged her own informed mind for Julia's less enquiring one at any price, but sometimes she could not help coveting Julia's beauty.

'That will do very well,' Julia said with a little, self-satisfied smile. 'I am sure Lewis will scarce be able to resist! After all, he has been away at sea a long time and must be delighted to gain some female companionship!'

Once again, Caroline felt the sharp, irrational pang of jealousy. Judging by Lewis Brabant's behaviour in the woods, she thought that Julia was probably right.

'Miss Brabant told me that Richard Slater has a sister,' she heard herself saying, 'so no doubt the Captain has had time to polish his address in Lyme before coming here!'

Julia gave her a sharp glare. 'I have met Fanny Slater, Caroline, and I do not think I need consider her a rival!' She smoothed the silk of her skirts with a loving hand. 'No indeed, she is a plain woman and has no conversation! And Lewis has already given the impression that he is more than glad to see me again…'

Caroline turned away to hide her face, busying her-self by straightening the pots and bottles on Julia's dressing-table. The room, decorated with swathes of pink satin and spindly white furniture, was a shrine to Julia's beauty.

'You are in earnest then, Julia? You wish to rekindle your romance with Captain Brabant?'

Julia shrugged carelessly. 'La, why not? It should provide some fun in this tediously dull place! Besides,' she gave Caroline a sparkling look, 'Lewis is rather attractive, is he not? He has changed since I met him last and I believe he could be quite a challenge! What do you think, Caroline?'

'I have no idea,' Caroline said sharply, bringing forward Julia's wrap. 'I am not accustomed to considering gentlemen in such way!'

'La, I should think not!' Julia's gaze was faintly malicious as it swept over her companion. 'That would be most inappropriate for a governess and could lead to all manner of difficulties! You will not be dining with us tonight,' she continued, taking the wrap without a word of thanks. 'You may take a tray in your room, Caroline. It is bad enough having to share Lewis's homecoming with that little milksop of a sister of his, without augmenting our party further!'

She let the wrap slide over her white arms and sighed. 'Lord, it is so slow living in the country! Now that Lewis is back I hope for some more invitations! I am sure that the Percevals will call, and perhaps even the Cleeves—did I tell you that I met the Countess in Town last year, Caroline, and she was most gracious to me! And now that we are neighbours...'

Caroline let the words flow over her head. She had heard quite enough of Julia's social pretensions in the last few weeks. The Cleeve and Perceval families had shown no inclination for a closer friendship with their neighbours at Hewly. They had been perfectly cordial on the few occasions that Julia and Caroline had encountered them in Abbot Quincey, but no invitations to visit had followed. When Julia had decided to call at Jaffrey House and Perceval Hall, the ladies were apparently not at home. Caroline had seen this as an unmistakable snub, but Julia had shrugged it off airily and persisted in her belief that they would all become great friends in time. For her part, Caroline suspected that the great families of the neighbourhood probably considered Julia encroaching and bad Ton, or even worse, not Ton at all.

'Speaking of the local aristocracy, I heard such a truly diverting piece of gossip this morning, Caro!' Julia spun round to fix her companion with bright, gleeful eyes. 'Only guess what has happened!'

Caroline bit her lip. 'I am sure that you will tell me—'

'Oh, you are so stuffy, pretending to a lack of interest! This is the most prime piece of news! The butcher's boy brought the story from the village—the *on dit* is that the Marchioness of Sywell has run away!'

Caroline stared. She remembered the notorious Marquis of Sywell from her time at the Guarding Academy, for his debauchery and wickedness had been a byword in the Abbey villages. Scarce a week had passed without his depravity being denounced in the local pulpits, rousing much speculation amongst the young ladies of the school as to the precise nature of the Marquis's iniquity. Once she had left the school, Caroline had gradually lost touch with the gossip of Steep Abbot and its environs, but on her return, Julia had been quick to update her on all of consequence. She had related the tale of the Marquis's ramshackle marriage with great excitement, but Caroline, deploring tittle-tattle, had not paid attention to half of it. Now it seemed that an even greater scandal had followed.

'The Marchioness?' Caroline said slowly. 'But surely you told me that they have been married for less than a year—'

Julia clapped her hands. 'I know! Is it not piquant! They said it would all end in tears, what with him being mad and thrice her age, and she being the strange creature she is!'

Caroline sat down on the end of the bed. 'Was she strange? I had not heard so—'

'Oh Caro, you must have heard the old story!' Julia looked eager. There was nothing she liked more than some scurrilous tale. 'Surely I told you already! The Marchioness was ward to the Abbey bailiff—or the bailiff's by-blow, more like! Do you not remember? John Hanslope went off in his cart one day and returned with a child! He said she was his ward and his wife educated her at home, for she had been a governess like yourself! We never saw hair nor hide of the girl—she never came into the village, or visited their neighbours, and you must concede that that is odd!'

Julia paused to adjust the bandeau restraining her curls, then resumed. 'I suppose you would not remember the chit's arrival, for it was just after your papa died and you had left Mrs Guarding's Academy. But surely I wrote to tell you all about it? I would *certainly* have written to relate so choice a piece of news!'

'I am sure you would,' Caroline murmured.

'Of course, at one time I was hoping to marry the Marquis myself,' Julia said brightly, peering into the mirror to view her reflection the better, 'but he was always a drunken old rake and Mrs B., the Admiral's wife, would not let me near him! Anyway, his taste obviously runs to the lower orders for the bailiff's ward to catch his notice!'

She picked up her reticule. 'I suppose the dinner gong will sound in a moment, but I must just finish the tale! When Mrs Hanslope, the bailiff's wife, died, he seemed uncertain of what to do with the girl and apprenticed her to some tradesman in Northampton, I believe, no doubt thinking that she might learn a useful profession! Anyway, she returned when Hanslope was on his deathbed, and made that shocking marriage to the Marquis! Scandalous!'

Caroline, remembering the spiteful delight with which Julia had imparted the tale of the Marquis's marriage, sighed a little. The Abbey villages had always been a hotbed of gossip—no doubt it was the same in any rural community—and probably there were precious few people with a kind word to say about the Marchioness.

'Where do they think she has gone?' she asked dubiously. 'With no friends and no one to help her—'

Julia shrugged carelessly. 'Heaven knows! But she is well served for her folly and greed, is she not! Presuming to marry a Marquis when she was a little nobody and probably quite unpresentable! No wonder that the villages can talk of little else!'

'What does Mr Hanslope have to say on all this?' Caroline asked slowly.

'Why, nothing! John Hanslope died a few months ago, just after the Marquis married his ward!' Julia said happily. 'Is it not the most *engrossing* tale, Caroline! Louise was her name. The bastard child of the bailiff! Each time Sywell did something outrageous they said that he could not possibly do worse, but of course he always did! And no doubt the girl was no better than she ought to have been, so there is one way that she might keep herself in the future—'

Caroline stood up. She had heard enough of Julia's spite. 'Well, it is an extraordinary tale, for sure, but—'

The gong sounded for dinner. Julia gave her golden curls one last, satisfied pat. 'There! I shall not be needing you again tonight, Caroline, for Letty will be back in time to help me undress.'

She swept out of the bedroom and down the curving stair. Caroline followed more slowly. Hewly Manor was a small house, dating in part from the fourteenth century, and whilst Julia deplored the inconvenience of the draughty old rooms and the lack of modern comforts, Caroline admired the style and elegance of previous centuries. The wooden stair led from the main landing directly down to the flagstone hall, where the dinner gong still reverberated softly. The Admiral had always insisted on military precision in his household and it was only recently, when his illness had become so much more severe, that standards had started to slip a little.

Julia grumbled that the food was always late and often cold, the service slipshod, and the servants paid her no heed. She felt was all of a piece with the dilapidation of the house and the estate, but Caroline's observation was that the servants were willing enough, but had no direction and no one to really care about them. She wondered what Lewis Brabant would make of all this neglect and reflected that she would not like to be in his servants' shoes. She already knew that Captain Brabant could be somewhat intimidating.

Caroline paused on the landing, taking care to stay well back in the shadows. She watched Julia descend slowly and saw her pause briefly before the long mirror that hung on the half-landing. Then, apparently satisfied with her appearance, she went down to join the Captain.

Caroline could see Lewis waiting at the bottom of the stair. The light fell on his upturned face as he watched Julia approach, and Caroline caught her breath. In his evening clothes, the dust from his journey washed away, he was elegance personified. The blue eyes that had regarded her so stonily earlier now

rested on Julia with warm appreciation. That firm
mouth held the hint of a disturbing smile. She saw
Lewis straighten up and step forward to take Julia's
hand. It was strange, but for a moment Caroline had
some impression of restlessness about him, as though
he already found the confines of the house chafing on
him. It was only a momentary feeling, but it made
Caroline wonder. A man who was used to the limit-
less expanse of the ocean could well find the boundaries of a country estate too restrictive.

'Good evening, Julia.' Caroline saw Lewis press a
kiss on Julia's hand. 'Lavender is already down, but
does Miss Whiston not join us for dinner?'

Caroline caught her breath. How would Julia re-
spond to that, when she had been the one to forbid
Caroline from accompanying them?

'Oh, Caro is a most retiring creature,' Julia said
with a ravishing smile, taking Lewis's arm. 'I tried to
persuade her to join us but she was positive in her
refusal! She is the most perfect companion, you
know, so discreet and unassuming. Now Lewis, I
want to hear all about your adventures! I am utterly
agog, my dear…'

The door of the drawing-room closed behind them.
Caroline felt an uncharacteristic urge to stamp her
foot. It was not that she had wished to take dinner
with the family, but overhearing Julia's misrepresen-
tations was too much. Even as a schoolgirl, Julia had
had an uncanny knack of twisting the truth to present
herself in the best possible light, and it seemed that
this ability had not diminished in time.

Caroline vented her feelings by slamming her bedroom door behind her. It was childish but it made her feel better. Normally she was capable of dismissing the slights and irritations of her working life. After all, she had endured many such in the time since she had left the Guarding Academy. For some reason, however, working at Hewly Manor was proving more difficult. Perhaps it was because she and Julia had once been friends but were now effectively mistress and servant; perhaps it was because of the memories stirred up by being in Steep Abbot again. And now, Caroline thought honestly, it was because of Lewis Brabant. Now that she had met him, she found she did not like the thought of Julia's plans of entrapment, which was odd, since she had dismissed the man as the veriest rake.

On impulse, Caro went across to her bed and pulled out the old carpet-bag that was hidden beneath. In it she kept her most treasured possessions. There were scant few: her book of sonnets, a fine gold pendant and matching brooch inherited from her mother, her grandfather's fob watch. There was also a pile of letters received from Julia over the years.

Julia's communications had been erratic. After she had married and moved from Steep Abbot she had not written for several years, but in her widowhood she had struck up a correspondence again. Caroline often wondered why she had bothered to keep the letters and had come to the conclusion that it was because they constituted a link with Steep Abbot and her childhood. Added to which, Julia's writing, whilst no great prose, was as entertaining as it was malicious.

Caroline turned to the early letters, the ones that Julia had sent when Caroline had taken up her first post as a governess in Yorkshire, and Julia had left the Guarding Academy and was living at Hewly under the chaperonage of the Honourable Mrs Brabant. She scanned the closely written lines until she found the bit that she was looking for.

'...Life is so dull now that you are gone, dearest Caro. Mrs B., whilst very amiable, is the most idle of creatures and will scarce take me anywhere! I am desperate for a season in Town! How else shall I find myself a husband? I shall end up setting my cap at Andrew, though he is the dullest of them all with his hunting and his fishing...'

Caroline raised her eyebrows. Andrew Brabant's dreariness had not prevented Julia from contracting an engagement to him at a later date. But that was not the bit that interested her—at least, not yet. Here it was:

'Lewis is down from Oxford,' she read. 'I believe he fancies himself as a poet, for he is most romantical, with a lock of hair falling into his eyes and a dreamy air. He is forever quoting verse and striking a pose. It would be fun to see if I could make him fall in love with me! That would be just the thing for a poet and might even improve his bad verse! Perhaps I shall try...

'You must remember Mrs Taperley, the farrier's wife? The *on dit* is that her new baby was fathered

by none other than the Marquis of Sywell—they say
the little boy is the very image! Mrs B. takes great
care to keep me out of Sywell's way, as you might
imagine, but I should rather like to catch a Marquis!

'The Admiral talks of nothing but this horrid War,
and is very dreary…'

There was more. Reams and reams of Julia's news
and gossip. Caroline skipped a couple of letters and
found another:

'Dearest Caro, the most diverting news! Lewis has
asked me to marry him! I knew I could bring him up
to scratch and indeed he is head over ears in love
with me! He is to go to sea and wished us to become
betrothed before he left. He is sure that the Admiral
will make no demur, and indeed he might not, for
have I not twenty thousand pounds? For my part, I
fear that Lewis may be away some time and cannot
imagine how I shall go on… I persuaded him that the
engagement should remain secret… I saw Hugo
Perceval in the village last week and thought him
most handsome…'

Caroline sighed. She stuffed the letters back in the
bag and pushed it out of sight under the bed. It
seemed that Lewis Brabant had only been the first of
Julia's conquests. It was not long before the
Admiral's ward had transferred her affections to the
older brother, and had entered into a more formal engagement. Julia had confided that the Admiral and his
wife had not liked the match above half, but that she
was determined to cut a dash in the neighbourhood
as Mrs Andrew Brabant. Alas for Julia, the plan had

been thwarted by the fever that carried off both Andrew and his mother, but it was not long before she had received an offer from Andrew's best friend, Jack Chessford... Jack had been handsome and rich, and Julia had achieved her aim of going to London at last. There had been no more letters until the one telling Caroline that Jack was dead in a carriage accident, the money was almost exhausted and Julia intended to make her home with her godfather, whose own health had deteriorated so markedly in recent years. Of Lewis, there had been no further mention at all.

That was until Caroline had come to Hewly to be Julia's companion. She shifted a little uncomfortably as she remembered how quickly she had got the measure of Julia's plans. As soon as Julia had discovered that Lewis Brabant was returning home, she declared that she intended to set her cap at him once more. Nor did she seem to see anything wrong in her plan to entrap him for her own amusement. Caroline sighed. Natural delicacy gave her an aversion to the idea, no matter how much she told herself that Lewis Brabant probably deserved such a fate, but she could scarcely warn him. Besides, Julia's feelings might be rather shallow at present, but it was not for Caroline to say that a deeper affection might not develop. She felt unaccountably depressed at the thought.

There was a knock at the door and Nurse Prior stuck her head round the door. A diminutive Yorkshirewoman, she had been nanny to all the Brabant children and had come out of retirement on the estate to nurse the Admiral after he was taken ill. Caroline and she had taken to each other quickly, each recognising the other's virtues. Mrs Prior had confided in an unguarded moment that Julia was about as much use as a chocolate fireguard, and had been appreciative of Caroline's help in the sickroom.

'Begging your pardon, Miss Whiston, but would you be so good as to sit with the Admiral for a little whilst I take my meal? The poor gentleman has not been so good today, and I don't like to leave him…'

Caroline jumped up. Over the past few weeks she had become accustomed to sitting with the Admiral whilst Mrs Prior took a rest. Julia never went near her godfather if she could help it, proclaiming herself too delicate for such unpleasantness, but Lavender, the Admiral's daughter, often took a turn to read to her father. Whether the Admiral was aware of any of them or not was a moot point. Often he would lie with his eyes open for hours on end, neither moving nor speaking. Sometimes he was voluble, but the words made little sense and he had to be soothed into a calmer frame of mind. If he were feeling well, he might get up and take a short turn about the garden, or sit in the drawing-room for a little, but he never gave any indication that he knew where he was or what was happening around him. Caroline, who remembered him from her youth as a strong, upright and active man, thought it a terrible pity.

The sickroom was in near-darkness, with only one candle burning on the table beside the bed. The Admiral lay on his back, gnarled hands resting on the coverlet, eyes closed. Caroline sat down beside the bed and picked up the book of naval stories that Lavender had evidently been reading earlier in the day. There was no sound but the Admiral's wheezing breath and the ticking of the clock on the mantelpiece. She started to read very softly.

Afterwards she could not believe that she had fallen asleep, but it had evidently been so, for she found that the book had slipped to her lap and her head had nodded forward. The candle had burned down a considerable way and the door was opening.

'I did not expect to find you here, ma'am.'

Caroline had been expecting Mrs Prior to return, but it was Lewis Brabant who now came forward into the glow of the candlelight. The flickering flame made him appear very tall and cast his face into shadow. He was still in his evening clothes and held a glass of brandy in one hand. Feeling suddenly flustered, Caroline got to her feet.

'Oh! Captain Brabant! Yes, I was sitting with your father whilst Mrs Prior had her dinner, but it seems—' She glanced at the clock in confusion, suddenly aware that it was much later than she had thought.

'The kitchen maid cut herself on the vegetable knife and Mrs Prior has been bandaging her up,' Lewis Brabant said with a smile. 'I am sorry that you have been delayed, Miss Whiston. I am happy to sit with my father for a little now, and allow you to join my sister and Mrs Chessford in the drawing-room.'

The prospect held little allure for Caroline, who could not think of many less enjoyable ways to finish the evening. Lewis was looking at his father's sleeping face and his expression was sombre.

'How has he been, Miss Whiston? Mrs Prior tells me that today has not been one of his better days.'

'The Admiral has been asleep whilst I have been here,' Caroline said, a little hesitantly. 'It is true that he has not stirred much today. Sometimes he is quite lively and even takes a walk in the gardens on fine days! And often he will talk to us—' She broke off, aware of Lewis Brabant's gaze resting on her face with disconcerting intentness.

'You must have spent a great deal of time with him,' he said. 'I thank you for that, Miss Whiston. It is kind of you.'

'Well...' Caroline found herself uncomfortable with his gratitude but did not wish to appear so ungracious as to dismiss it. People so seldom thanked her for anything she did. Besides, it was true that caring for the Admiral was not a part of her duties and she had undertaken it to help Mrs Prior and Lavender.

'Mrs Prior is a devoted nurse,' she said guardedly, 'but even she needs a rest occasionally. I believe she would work her fingers to the bone otherwise!'

'She was always the same,' Lewis said, smiling ruefully. 'Did Nanny Prior tell you that she was nurse to us all, and to my mother's family before that? She has always been a tower of strength.'

He moved across to the fire and banked it up. The flames shot up and sent the shadows dancing along the wall. Caroline felt suddenly faint with hunger and grasped the chair back to steady herself. She had forgotten that she had not yet eaten and that the hour for dinner was long past.

'I do believe that you must have missed your dinner, ma'am,' Lewis Brabant said, straightening up and coming towards her, concern showing on his face. He took her arm. 'You look quite pale! Stay here whilst I go to order you a tray of food. We cannot do with having to call Dr Pettifer out for you as well!'

'I am very well, I thank you, sir,' Caroline said, her face flaming with embarrassment. The hard strength of his hand under her arm was strangely disturbing. She felt her head spin with a combination of hunger and mortification, and Lewis gave an exclamation and pressed the brandy glass into her hand.

'Here, take this, Miss Whiston, before you swoon! You will find it most efficacious!'

He was right. The strong spirit burned Caroline's throat and made her cough a little, but the world immediately came back into closer focus. She looked a little doubtfully from the empty glass to Lewis's smiling face.

'Thank you, sir... Your best brandy! I am so sorry—'

Lewis shrugged gracefully. 'It is of no consequence, Miss Whiston! I will fetch another glass.' His amused scrutiny dwelled on her face, which had gone from chalk white to rosy pink. 'I believe that you should retire to your room until I can arrange for a tray to be brought up. For those unaccustomed to strong liquor the result can be confusing!'

'I am not unaccustomed to brandy,' Caroline began, then realised how her words must sound and broke off in confusion. 'That is, I have drunk it before... My grandfather used to promote it as medicinal against chills...' She realised that she was rambling. Lewis had raised one eyebrow and was watching her with a quizzical amusement that disconcerted her.

'I thought for a moment that you must be one of those fabled governesses who was addicted to drink, Miss Whiston!' he said mildly. 'Such an idea seems absurd, but one must always expect the unexpected...'

The colour flooded Caroline's face again. On an empty stomach the drink was proving as much a curse as a blessing. She extricated herself carefully from Lewis's grip and walked towards the door.

'Pray do not trouble yourself to arrange any food for me, sir. I shall go down to the kitchens directly.'

Lewis shrugged, opening the door for her. 'Very well, Miss Whiston. I can see that you mean to be confoundedly independent!' His gaze travelled over her thoughtfully. 'I see also that you have rejected your red velvet for more sober garb! How very apt for a governess companion!'

Caroline looked up at him. The faint light could not hide the mockery in his eyes.

'I am persuaded,' he added pleasantly, 'that it can only be skin deep, however! The dryad who walks the woods reading verse must be the real Miss Whiston! The child who was brought up on brandy-drinking...'

'The real Miss Whiston has a living to earn,' Caroline said tartly, 'and has no time for conundrums, sir! Pray excuse me!'

Lewis Brabant gave her an ironic bow. 'Do not let me keep you from your duties then, ma'am! Good night!'

Caroline closed the door softly behind her and leant against the jamb for a moment to steady herself. It seemed that Lewis Brabant, despite his admiration for Julia, was not above flirting with the companion. Such behaviour was not unfamiliar to Caroline, for she had met plenty of men who thought that governesses and companions were fair game for their advances. Normally such situations gave her no trouble but what was particularly confusing here was her own reaction to Lewis. She should have given him a sharp setdown, but instead she had felt a treacherous attraction, as bewildering as it was unwelcome.

She went slowly down the stairs, through the door to the servants' quarters and along the corridor to the kitchen. The chatter and light interrupted her thoughts, but as she sat down at the trestle table and accepted a bowl of soup, she could not help but wonder just what Lewis Brabant thought of her. Then she thought that perhaps his mind was so full of Julia that he did not think of her at all, and she found that that was more annoying still.

Lewis waited until the door had closed behind Caroline, then took the chair beside the bed, sat back and closed his eyes. It had been a long day and he was bone weary, but despite that, he had to fight a strong urge to take a horse to the Admiralty and demand to be given the first ship available.

His responsibilities dragged him down like lead weights. The house was in poor condition and the estate even more so. His father's man of business had been blunt about the time and effort it would take to get things back into shape and Lewis was not sure that he even wanted to try. He had little affinity with a place that he had only visited once in the past ten years. As Richard had pointed out, it was not even near the sea! If it had not been for his family…

Lewis opened his eyes. His father's breathing was steady but the old man showed no flicker of consciousness. Lewis was aware of a profound sadness. It could only be a matter of time before the Admiral passed on, but he owed it to his father to see that his last days were as comfortable as possible. He would have to talk to the doctor in the morning.

Lewis leant forward and looked at his father's sleeping face. They had never been particularly close, but the Admiral had been a fair man and they had respected each other. Harley Brabant had never understood his son's bookish tendencies but had tolerated them whilst complaining that Lewis took after his mother's side of the family. All the same, Lewis knew that his father had been very proud when he had chosen to follow him into the Navy. It was comforting to think that the Admiral had approved of him.

Which was why... Lewis sighed. Which was why it was difficult to escape the notion that the Admiral would wish his son to continue what he had begun at Hewly Manor. Lewis knew that he could always sell up and move away, but he could not escape the thought that this would be going against the Admiral's wishes.

Then there was Lavender. His sister had only been fourteen when he had gone away and Lewis was uncomfortably aware that she was now a grown woman who must have her own hopes and aspirations. He barely knew her and she was a reserved character who might take some time to understand. He had already seen that she disliked Julia...

Lewis shifted slightly. Julia was just as he remembered her, only more beautiful, sweeter, more desirable. She had been eighteen when he had gone to sea, and he a youth of twenty-two who had thought himself so worldly wise and brave! A faint smile twisted his lips. What a lot he had learned in those first few months, racked by seasickness and homesickness in equal measure, afraid and forlorn! The lowest point had been when he had received his mother's letter telling him of Julia's betrothal to his brother. Lewis had felt sick and betrayed, for had not Julia exchanged the most tender vows with him, promising to wait for him for ever?

He had been prepared to put such youthful folly behind him on his return to Hewly. After all, he and Julia were ten years older and such boy and girl affairs were best left in the past. But to his amazement, there had been a letter from Julia awaiting him on his arrival in London, explaining that she had felt it her duty to return to Hewly to care for the Admiral. She expressed herself delighted to be able to welcome him back to his old home. Her words were well chosen and gracious, and had stirred in him a faint but definite anticipation at seeing her again. And then they had met…

Lewis got up and walked over to the window. The heavy velvet curtains had been drawn against the November dark, and when he pushed them back he felt the cold air rush into the overheated sickroom. The moon was high and cast a silver shadow over the deserted garden. He felt restless and cooped up in the house. With a sigh, Lewis let the curtain fall back into place and moved over to the fire. He had imagined that there might be some initial awkwardness in meeting Julia again, but this had proved far from the case. She had been the perfect hostess, but with added warmth that had been most encouraging.

Thinking of Julia led him to think of Caroline Whiston. There was an enigma. No warm welcome from her! For a moment, Lewis recalled the tantalising softness of Caroline in his arms, her lips parting beneath his. The change from that spirit of the woods into the severe companion in her drab worsted was almost unbelievable. It was as though she deliberately hid a part of herself away. Yet she was not ill-looking. It was almost as though she deliberately sought to efface herself, hiding that glorious chestnut hair, choosing colours that drained all vitality from her pale complexion, concealing her figure. It had not been hidden in that red velvet dress... Lewis smothered a grin. Nor could Miss Whiston disguise the flashing beauty of those hazel eyes. She was a most unusual lady's companion indeed.

Lewis stirred the fire, still thinking of her. What on earth had possessed him to accost her in that particular way? True, he had thought her a maidservant or village girl when he had first glimpsed her, but he was hardly the man to go around stealing kisses from servants! There had been some affinity, some instant chemistry between them that had leapt into immediate life. He was certain she felt it too, for later she had been nervous of him, reserved. Stern Miss Whiston would never allow him within arm's length again!

Lewis sighed, his conscience pricking him. It was little wonder that Miss Whiston had been nervous after his behaviour earlier in the day. Companions and governesses were in a vulnerable position and he had taken advantage. Yet there was something about the girl that drew him on...

'Petticoat government!' Richard Slater had commented, on hearing that Lewis would be returning to a house full of women. Lewis grimaced. He would have to change that. Already he felt stifled by the claustrophobic atmosphere of Hewly Manor, the shadow of the sickroom, the circumscribed life of the country. He would write to Richard and ask him to bring a party to Hewly, then he would throw himself into the management of the estate, visit his neighbours, find somehow, the piece of his life that seemed to be missing. Previously, it had been the Navy that had filled the spaces in his life, occupying his time and energies. It was his main love, but if there was to be another… His thoughts turned fleetingly to Julia again. His first love. The thought of her as a country wife was laughable, but for the time being at least they were sharing a house and he was still not sure if he was glad or sorry. He picked up the brandy glass and looked at it thoughtfully. He must ask Caroline Whiston more about the grandfather who had encouraged brandy-drinking as a cure for chills. Thinking of her once more, Lewis took the empty glass and went downstairs in search of a refill.

Chapter Three

There were no more early morning walks for Caroline. The weather had turned wet and windy and, even had she wanted to venture out, Julia kept her busier than ever with a wealth of trivial little jobs. She saw little of Lewis Brabant, for he spent most of his days immured with his estate manager or riding out to inspect the property, returning only for dinner. Caroline never ate with the family and made sure that she avoided Lewis if it was at all possible. Nevertheless she found herself curiously aware of his presence, as though the house was alive with a new energy.

From what little she did see of him, it struck Caroline that Lewis was a very self-contained man. He listened carefully, spoke sparingly, watched intently and missed very little of what went on. She noticed him taking particular pains to draw Lavender out and was amused to see that whilst his sister's natural reserve kept her quiet to begin with, she was soon responding to his genuine interest. Caroline thought that Lavender had probably been lonely and the return of her brother was just what she needed. Julia had never troubled to befriend her and Caroline had suspected that Lavender did not like her anyway, although Miss Brabant was far too well bred to give any indication of her feelings. To Caroline, Lavender had always been pleasant but very quiet, and because she avoided Julia, Caroline had never had the chance to progress the acquaintance. Now though, under Lewis's encouragement, Caroline saw that Lavender was emerging from her shell.

She found the two of them together in the library one morning when Julia had sent her downstairs to choose her a book. The fair heads were bent close together over what looked like an estate map, and Caroline paused on the threshold, reflecting on the strong family likeness and not wishing to intrude. Then Lewis looked up, tossed her a charming smile and rolled the map up.

'Miss Whiston! How are you, ma'am? My sister has just been showing me her sketches—she has been drawing flora over by Steepwood Lawn. Do you know that part of the forest at all from your walks?'

His tone was suspiciously bland, but since Steepwood Lawn was close to where the two of them had met on his first day home, Caroline knew that he must be teasing her. To her vexation, she felt the faint colour come into her cheeks. Lewis's gaze was bright with amusement as it rested on her face, one brow quirked in enquiry, his blue eyes dancing.

'I believe I know the place a little,' Caroline said stiffly. She saw that Lavender was watching her with a gaze as perceptive as her brother's and tried to overcome her discomfort. 'Will you show me your sketches, Miss Brabant? I should like to see them very much.'

'Of course,' Lavender murmured, gesturing towards the pencil drawings scattered across the table.

Caroline looked, and forgot her self-consciousness. 'But these are beautiful!' she exclaimed warmly. 'I did not realise that you could draw so well, Miss Brabant!' She leant closer. 'And unless I mistake, that is a May Lily! I had no notion that they grew in the woods hereabouts!'

Lavender's eyes lit up. '*Maianthemum bifolium*; you are not mistaken, Miss Whiston, though they are rare. They prefer a light acid soil, you see, and only grow in certain parts of the forest.'

'And oxlip, and squill...' Caroline smiled as she drew the sheets towards her. 'It is a while since I studied botany, but—'

'You studied botany?' Lavender's face was eager. She looked animated and very pretty. Caroline, remembering how Julia had always dismissed Lavender's fair looks as insipid, realised that they had all underestimated the younger girl. She smiled shamefacedly. 'Well, my studies were only for my own enjoyment and most amateur! But I have a delightful book inherited from my grandpapa! It contains all the wild flowers and a wealth of detail. If you would like to borrow it—'

She broke off, aware that Lewis Brabant was watching her, a smile in his eyes. It made her feel as though the room was suddenly overheated. She looked hastily away. Fortunately Lavender appeared not to have noticed.

'Oh, Miss Whiston, thank you! That would be most pleasant!'

Lewis Brabant strode forward with a lazy grace. 'It will be good for you to have another expert to talk to, Lavender, rather than a brother who is a dullard!'

Lavender laughed. 'No such thing, Lewis! You are ridiculous!'

'Well, I assure you I cannot tell a petal from a stamen, but I do know that your drawings are very fine! Now, you must excuse me for I must be about estate business.' He paused with his hand on the door-handle. 'You will not forget the commission at Hammond's for me, Lavender? Perhaps Miss Whiston might accompany you if she has any errands into Abbot Quincey?'

Caroline agreed readily. 'I have some ribbons to buy for Mrs Chessford and a number of small purchases to make. If you do not mind waiting whilst I choose another book…'

She put the two volumes she was carrying down on the table and moved across to the oaken shelves to choose something else for Julia. Lewis picked up the books and perused their spines. He looked at her quizzically.

'*Sense and Sensibility* and *Marmion*! A curious mixture, Miss Whiston!'

'Oh,' Caroline felt flustered. '*Sense and Sensibility* is Mrs Chessford's choice—'

Lewis raised his eyebrows. 'You do surprise me, ma'am! So Julia reads the books on manners and morals, and you read the romance! How singular, when outward appearances would suggest otherwise!'

He put the book in his pocket. 'I should like to read *Marmion* again…' He raised a hand in farewell. 'You must join us for dinner tonight, Miss Whiston. No more skulking in your room!' And he left Caroline feeling confused and annoyed, and suspicious that she had glimpsed more than a hint of speculation in Lavender's eyes.

The walk to Abbot Quincey was very pleasant, though the roads were a little muddy after the recent rain. It was the first fine day of the week, and Julia had roused herself sufficiently to take the carriage and go to visit friends near Northampton. She had dismissed Caroline, telling her that she did not need her when there was other, more congenial company to be had, which left her companion feeling more than ever sorry to be the butt of Julia's bad manners.

Lavender Brabant was a different matter, however, and there was certainly no faulting her courtesy. They talked of botany and art as they walked, and found that they had plenty of interests in common to make the journey pass quickly. Lavender's companionship was stimulating after Julia's trivial gossip, and Caroline felt her spirits lift at being out in the fresh air. They reached Abbot Quincey to find that it was busy, despite not being a market day, and strolled down the main street to pause before Hammond's general store and admire the new frontage. Lavender giggled over the fanlight and huge bow windows.

'Oh dear, it looks a little excessive for a country town! I understand that Mr Hammond has modelled it on his store in Northampton, and is as proud as proud! Only look, dear Miss Whiston—he has festooned the doorway with his muslin and kerseymere! I do so hope he will not get mud on it!'

They were about to enter the shop when they were hailed from close quarters by a cadaverous gentleman with an eager eye. Lavender gave Caroline a speaking glance, ducked under the swathes of drapery and disappeared into Hammond's interior. Caroline sighed and turned to greet the newcomer, trying to compose her face into an expression that was pleasant without being too welcoming.

'Mr Grizel. How do you do, sir?'

Hubert Grizel was curate of a neighbouring parish and had recently preached at the church in Abbot Quincey, on the invitation of the Reverend William Perceval. From the moment Caroline had seen him in church, she had identified him as the perfect example of a worthy clergyman looking for a consort. From the moment he had clapped eyes on Caroline, it was evident that Mr Grizel thought that he had found her. He had called at Hewly, not once but several times, and Julia had made sport of his pastoral visits until Caroline was very uncomfortable. She had no wish to encourage the cleric, but equally no desire to embarrass him.

'Miss Whiston!' Mr Grizel's thin face flushed with

pleasure. He removed his hat, gave a gallant bow and looked as though he were about to topple over. 'How are you, ma'am? You look very well, if I may make so bold! I had been intending to call at Hewly, but the weather being as it has—' He gestured vaguely towards the muddy road.

Caroline smiled. 'I am very well, I thank you, sir, as are all at the Manor. There has been little change in the Admiral's condition. But you will perhaps have heard our good news? Captain Brabant is returned—'

Mr Grizel had indeed heard all about Lewis Brabant's return. 'I am relieved that the Captain is home safely from the wars,' he observed pompously, 'and am more than ever comforted that you ladies are no longer unprotected. A house full of women is in need of a staunch defender!'

Caroline repressed the urge to tell him that they had scarcely felt in danger before, and a small silence fell. It was clear that Mr Grizel was trying to think of some conversational topic and equally clear that Caroline did not intend to help him.

'Well,' Caroline said brightly after a moment, gesturing towards the shop, 'I must be about my errands! We will see you again soon, Mr Grizel.'

Mr Grizel ardently assured her that she would indeed, and took himself off, still stammering profuse compliments.

Caroline smiled a little as she negotiated the blue spotted muslin adorning Hammond's doorway. Poor Mr Grizel! She hoped that she had mistaken his intentions but suspected that she had read them all too clearly. He could scarcely be blamed for considering a governess companion as a suitable wife and she just hoped she had not been so civil as to encourage his pretensions. She had no wish to hurt his feelings.

The interior of the shop was dark after the sunshine outside, and Caroline paused to allow her eyes to attune. One half of the shop was a grocery and general store, selling everything from candles to teapots, whilst the other half was a drapers. It was clear that Arthur Hammond was not a man to miss a commercial opportunity. He understood perfectly that his country clients could be anyone from the baker's wife to Lady Perceval, and that rich and poor alike required a shop that sold all the bits and pieces they needed to save them making the journey into Northampton. At the same time he managed to give the impression of fine quality. Local gossip said that Hammond was very rich and an inveterate social climber, and Caroline could well believe it. She knew that he owned an emporium in Northampton and a string of other shops in the county, and that other members of his family had also made a fortune from trade. Hammond's children had been sent away to get a fine education, all except Barnabas, his eldest son, who was being groomed to take over the shop.

Caroline ducked behind a bolt of glossy lustring that was resting against the shelves, and looked around for the ribbons. Julia had asked her to match some colours for two new gowns. She had chosen the dress material herself, but had lost interest in the details once the purchase was made, leaving the choice to her companion. Caroline did not mind. She knew she had a good eye for colour and style when given a chance, and if Julia did not like the outcome she should not have delegated the task in the first place.

Caroline paused before a display of fine stockings and lace. Would that she had either the opportunity or the means to wear such clothes! The red dress was the only luxurious item of clothing that she possessed, and she had ruthlessly avoided buying clothes she had known she would never wear. Nevertheless it would be fun one day... Caroline caught herself in a rosy dream where she was dressed in green silk and descending a sweeping staircase to a ballroom... She put it firmly from her mind.

She caught sight of Lavender over by the counter, purchasing some gold braid, presumably the commission from Lewis. Barnabas Hammond himself was attending to her, which struck Caroline as interesting since the purchase was small enough for one of the assistants to attend her. Lavender's head was bent over her purse and there was an expression in Barnabas's eyes that made Caroline's heart skip a beat. So the draper's handsome son had a *tendre* for the Admiral's daughter! Caroline watched as Lavender looked up, met Barney's very dark eyes and blushed becomingly. She pursed her lips in silent surprise. So the interest was mutual! Caroline could not be surprised, for any woman could see that Barney Hammond was a devastatingly attractive man. And perhaps it was simply a physical attraction on Lavender's part. She had probably not met many young men and Barney had a strong, lithe physique, and a dark, intense gaze that was particularly compelling. Village gossip had it that the girls were mad for him, but Barney was quiet and kept himself to himself, almost as much as Lavender did…

Barney looked up, saw Caroline watching and straightened up, taking a step backwards and assuming a more formal expression. Caroline hurried forward with her fabric samples. She liked Barney and did not wish to be thought prying, but she could not help but wonder how Lewis would feel if his sister had developed a genuine affection for the draper's son. For all Arthur Hammond's pretensions, it could not be seen as an equal match.

With ribbons, buttons and braid purchased, and waved on their way by a fulsome Arthur Hammond himself, Caroline and Lavender stepped out into Abbot Quincey's main street once more. There was a delicate flush still on Lavender's high cheekbones and a sparkle in her eyes, but before Caroline could decide whether or not to quiz her, they bumped into Lady Perceval.

Caroline felt a little awkward. The last time she had met Lady Perceval and her daughters she had been with Julia, and whilst they had all exchanged cordial greetings, it had seemed clear to Caroline that the Percevals had no wish to further the acquaintance. This was a little odd, for Caroline knew Lady Perceval to be the kindest of creatures and her generosity was spoken of very highly in the neighbourhood. Caroline had been forced to draw the unhappy

conclusion that it was Julia who was the rub and that
Lady Perceval did not wish to encourage her. This
opinion was now borne out as her ladyship greeted
Lavender very warmly.

'My dear! How delightful to see you again!' She
took Lavender's hand in hers and bent a friendly
smile on Caroline. 'And Miss Whiston! A pleasure!'
She turned back to Lavender. 'We were so pleased to
hear of your brother's return, Miss Brabant! You must
be greatly relieved to have him home.'

Lavender blushed and smiled. 'Oh, Lady Perceval,
it is indeed a pleasure to have Lewis back! I have
missed him a great deal!'

Lady Perceval patted her hand. 'Very natural, my
dear! I hope that he will settle to life in the neighbourhood—we all do! It will be good for the estate.'
A frown of concern touched her brow. 'And your father? How is he?'

Lavender seemed to droop a little. 'I fear he is not
well, Lady Perceval. I do not believe it can be long—'
She broke off. 'It makes me more grateful than ever
to have my brother home.'

Lady Perceval sighed. 'Yes, indeed. It is fortunate
that you have his support at so difficult a time.' She
turned to Caroline. 'It is good to see you back in
Northamptonshire too, Miss Whiston. You must see
some changes since your time at the school!'

'I do indeed, ma'am, I thank you,' Caroline murmured, surprised at this sign of notice. She had not
realised that Lady Perceval even knew who she was,
let alone her past history.

Lady Perceval was still smiling at her. 'I knew your mama, you know, Miss Whiston. We were débutantes together, Deborah and I.' She sighed and shook her head. 'She was a good friend and I am sorry that we lost touch with each other. If you are ever in need of any help—' suddenly there was significant look in Lady Perceval's eye '—I beg you to come to me. I should do my best to assist you.'

She smiled at Lavender again. 'Well, I should not keep you. No doubt your brother will have a hundred and one things to do about the estate, Miss Brabant, but Sir James and I should be pleased if the two of you would care to dine at the Hall one evening. I will send the invitation over. Good day, Miss Brabant.' She nodded to Caroline. 'Miss Whiston.'

'How charming of her,' Lavender said, as they set off to walk back to Steep Abbot. 'I must confess that I have little taste for company, but the Percevals have always been very amiable to me.' A cloud touched her face. 'Julia will not be pleased, I fear, but Lady Perceval made no mention of including her in the invitation!'

Caroline hesitated. She would have put it far more strongly and observed that Lady Perceval had pointedly excluded Julia from the invitation to dine. She could hardly say so, however. Julia was her employer and as such she owed her discretion at least.

Lavender touched her arm in a contrite fashion.

'I do apologise, Miss Whiston! It must be difficult enough for you, without my tactless remarks! Let us not speak of Julia and spoil this lovely day!'

Caroline's lips twitched. Despite herself, it was diverting to be sympathised with for putting up with Julia Chessford. More than ever, Julia seemed like the cuckoo in the nest at Hewly, unwelcome but somehow too important to be dislodged. But of course, all that would change if she married Lewis. Mrs Lewis Brabant could hardly be ignored in the neighbourhood. It seemed to Caroline as though the sun had suddenly gone behind a cloud.

'Lady Perceval was very gracious to you too, was she not, Miss Whiston?' Lavender commented. 'I had no idea that she knew your family! But what did she mean by offering her help to you should you need it?'

'I imagine that she thought I might need some assistance in finding a new position one day,' Caroline said neutrally, wondering if that was what had really prompted Lady Perceval's words. 'It is very kind of her.'

'Oh, she is the soul of kindness!' Lavender agreed. 'I suppose that she could be in the right of it, if Julia moved away, or were to marry…'

Caroline decided to change the subject. She did not want to dwell on Julia's matrimonial plans a second longer. Knowing that Julia was making a dead set for Lewis put her in a very awkward position when speaking to Lewis's sister. With a sigh, Caroline reflected that the lot of a governess was preferable to that of a companion. She already felt that she was the repository of too many difficult secrets.

'I am glad you are so pleased to have your brother

back at home, Miss Brabant,' she said warmly. 'Do you see much of a change in him?'

Lavender smiled, and it lit up her whole face. 'To tell the truth, Miss Whiston, I do not really remember what Lewis was like before he went to sea. He was very much the older brother, you see, although not as distant as Andrew, of course!' She gave a peal of laughter. 'I do remember that he was very affected when he returned from University—he used to write very bad poetry and was forever striking a tragic pose until one wished to shake him, but I believe the Navy must have discouraged such foolishness in him! At any rate, he is much more forceful and decisive than I remember him, which is little wonder.' She hesitated. 'I do question how it must be for him to return home, however. Hewly is hardly a happy place with my father so ill and the estate gone to ruin. I wonder if Lewis will not simply sell up and return to sea in time…'

Caroline was startled. 'But Hewly is a sound estate and surely must return a profit once it is in better repair! And your brother would not wish to remain at sea forever—' She broke off, realising that she must sound presumptuous.

Lavender did not appear to mind. 'I may be mistaken, but I do not think that Hewly holds happy memories for Lewis. Besides, it is not as though Hewly is a family home in the sense of Perceval Hall. Papa purchased the house, but you must know, Miss Whiston, that his family seat is in Yorkshire. As a younger son, however, he had his own way to make.

Mama, of course, was one of the Fontenoys, but for all her aristocratic connections she had no money, so—' she shrugged '—Hewly should have become our family home. Fate has decreed that it is not a lucky one.'

'Neither for you nor your brother,' Caroline said sympathetically. 'You do not mention your own situation, Miss Brabant, but I imagine that it cannot always have been happy.'

Lavender coloured a little. 'Oh, I manage as well I might. I have been fortunate in spending time in Town with Aunt Augusta Carew—she even sponsored me in society, you know, Miss Whiston, and was very put out that I did not take!' There was suddenly a mischievous look in Lavender's eye that reminded Caroline forcibly of Lewis. 'It is not fashionable to admit it, but I prefer the country to Town. I had no time for all those fops and dandies, and silly, empty-headed girls who had no interest but to catch a rich husband!'

Caroline burst out laughing. 'And I admire you for it, Miss Brabant! The pleasures of drawing and botany must far outweigh those of balls and parties!'

'Why, so I think!' Lavender said spontaneously. 'Although—' a wistful note entered her voice '—I did enjoy the theatre and some of the balls…'

'Perhaps your brother will take a house in Town for the season next year,' Caroline suggested. 'It would be just the thing for you all…'

'I am sure he will do if Cousin Julia has any say in the matter.' Suddenly there was a different note in

Lavender's voice. 'I do so hope that Lewis will not—'
She broke off abruptly. 'I beg your pardon, Miss
Whiston. I have run on a great deal, which is most
unlike me!'

'Pray do not apologise,' Caroline said with a smile.
'It is very pleasant to have your conversation, Miss
Brabant.'

'Then will you not call me Lavender?' the younger
girl said, a little hesitantly. 'I should so like us to be
friends…'

Caroline was touched. 'Well, only if you will call
me Caroline,' she temporised. 'Since we are to be
friends and we share a home, at least for the time
being.'

'I should like that,' Lavender agreed smilingly. 'Oh
look, I do believe that is Lewis approaching—'

They both spun around at the sound of wheels
along the track behind them. Lewis Brabant was driv-
ing towards them and for some reason the sight of
him made Caroline blush, as though she had been
caught out in some misdemeanour. She stepped on to
the grass verge and was about to suggest to Lavender
that Lewis take her up in the gig for the rest of the
journey home, when Lavender said hastily, 'You must
be tired with carrying that heavy basket, Caroline!
Lewis can take you up and I shall cut across the fields
here…' And almost before she had finished, she was
through the gate and away. Caroline stared after her
in perplexity. Lavender, it seemed, had a mysterious
habit of appearing and disappearing like a will-o'-
the-wisp.

Lewis Brabant pulled the gig up beside Caroline a moment later. 'Miss Whiston! I looked for you both in Abbot Quincey, but it seems that I must have just missed you! Is everything all right, ma'am? My sister seemed in an unconscionable hurry to escape!'

Caroline's eyebrows were still raised at Lavender's hasty departure. Neither their conversation nor Lewis's arrival seemed to require such speed and she was at a loss to explain it.

'I think Miss Brabant preferred to walk back across the fields,' she said, lightly. 'I believe she might have in mind some scene for a new sketch!'

Lewis Brabant gave her a rueful smile. He jumped down on to the road. 'No doubt! And in the meantime, you are left with the heavy basket! You must let me take you up, ma'am! It will save you a good half-mile!'

Caroline hung back, unwilling to analyse why she felt so reluctant to join him in the gig. 'Oh, but have you finished your business about the estate? I have no wish to inconvenience you, and the basket is really very light—'

Lewis had already taken it from her arm and now had his hand under her elbow, ready to help her climb up into the cart. Before Caroline could even finish her sentence, she found herself installed on the bench with a rug tucked around her.

'It is not so dashing as a phaeton,' Lewis said with a smile as he swung up beside her, 'but a deal more practical on these roads! I would take Nelson out, but he is still a little lame. Thank you for tending to him the day that I arrived, Miss Whiston.' He flashed her a glance. 'The groom told me that you had given very clear instructions on what was wrong with his leg. Do you ride, Miss Whiston?'

'I used to ride as a girl,' Caroline admitted, trying not to smile at the thought of a horse named after England's greatest Admiral of recent times, 'and I enjoyed it a great deal. There has been little call for it in my various posts, however!'

Lewis encouraged the horses to a stately trot. There was little room on the bench, and Caroline jumped as his body brushed against hers. It filled her with an odd feeling of awareness.

'Have you always lived in the country, ma'am, or did the families you lived with sometimes go to Town?'

Caroline tried to concentrate. 'Oh, I have lived mainly in the country and like your sister, I much prefer it! I had a season in Town when I was young—' she hesitated, not wishing to sound as though she were complaining of her lot '—before my father died.'

'Did you so?' Lewis shot her a quick sideways look. His gaze was frankly admiring and brought further colour to her cheeks. 'I am surprised you did not make a match of it! You must have had plenty of offers!'

The breeze cooled Caroline's hot face. 'I did not take,' she said lightly, remembering Lavender's words of ten minutes before. 'I was a hoyden in those days and the stately dowagers took me in dislike!

Fortunately I did not know what would shortly befall me—'

She broke off, aware that her words were equivocal. She did not wish to imply that she would have made a marriage of convenience, for she would have done no such thing. What she had meant was that she had been a heedless girl who had grown up swiftly when she had been forced to earn her own living. There was no way that Lewis would realise that, however.

'I suppose that an expedient marriage would have been a preferable alternative to having to earn a living—' Lewis too broke off, seeing Caroline's discomfort, and for a moment there was a constrained silence broken only by the clatter of the horses' hooves on the track.

Caroline felt awkward. He had misunderstood her in precisely the way she had feared, thinking that she would have accepted any offer to escape penury. She did not like to think that he would believe her shallow enough to consider such a course of action. For some reason it seemed important to correct his impression, but she hesitated on the edge of explaining, good manners holding her back. Whilst she struggled with her feelings, Lewis spoke again.

'I beg your pardon, Miss Whiston,' he said slowly. 'I should not have spoken thus. I fear I am not accustomed to having to choose my words with such care as society requires. I meant no offence.'

'I imagine that one would run aground if procrastination were the rule at sea,' Caroline said brightly.

She found she could not look at him. Her overriding thought was that now he must believe her superficial indeed. She closed her eyes. Why his good opinion should matter so much was unclear, but matter it did.

'So Lavender prefers the country to the city, does she?' Lewis said, after a brief moment. 'I had guessed as much, but was not sure if she was secretly hankering for another season in Town! I had thought to take a house there next year, but I believe the estate will demand so much of my time that it may not be possible for a while.'

'Has the estate fallen into disrepair so very quickly, then?' Caroline asked, hoping that her interest would not be construed as impertinence. 'I did not think that the Admiral had been ill for so very long—'

'It is true that he only had his attack three months ago,' Lewis agreed, 'but I believe his health has been in decline ever since my mother died. They were most sincerely attached. Then there was the blow of losing my brother as well. I believe he felt that all he had worked for was slipping away and that he started to let it go as of that time.'

'I am sorry,' Caroline said hesitantly, 'and for yourself also, having to return from sea at such a time…'

'Well,' Lewis turned his head and gave her a slight smile, 'I was due to return shortly anyway, although the circumstances were not what I would have chosen. My last ship, *Dauntless*, was to be scrapped and they had not yet assigned me to another. A pity,' he added absently, his eyes on the road. 'She was a fine vessel, brave and true…'

They had reached a bend in the road where the land fell away to the south and Hewly could be seen nestling in its hollow, the village of Steep Abbot curled around. The river lay like a shining ribbon and the forest spread away beyond the fields like a patchwork quilt. Caroline could not help a smile.

'It is so very beautiful, though, is it not, Captain Brabant? If one must be forced to stay on land one could do worse! The house is a little gem—it is full of unique features! Did you know that the plaster representations on the wall in the porch are very rare? I have been reading up on their history, and—' She stopped, suddenly self-conscious, wondering why she was rattling on to him about his own home. No doubt he knew far more about it than she! Lewis was smiling too. He gave the horse the office to move off again. 'You must tell me about the history of the Manor some time, Miss Whiston,' he said pleasantly. 'I confess I know little of it, though I suspect Lavender is well-read on the subject! She seems to have a very well-informed mind.'

'Your sister is a very accomplished girl,' Caroline agreed, secretly glad to turn the subject. She was not sure what was the matter with her, only that she seemed as awkward as a green girl in his company. 'Mrs Guarding's school deserves its good reputation.'

'Yet more than a good education must be required for a cultivated mind, surely,' Lewis observed. 'There must be an interest, a willingness to learn…'

Caroline tried not to think of Julia, who had to be the best example of an uncultivated mind and wasted education that she could imagine. 'I believe Miss Brabant possesses both,' she said carefully.

'And I am grateful that she has sensible company here at Hewly, ma'am!' Lewis gave her a warm smile. 'Lavender was ever a quiet child. The gap in age between the three of us was enough to set her apart, leaving aside the difference of her sex. I had feared she might become a recluse, but I realise that your presence here must be of great benefit to her.'

Caroline felt warmed by his approval and told herself severely not to be foolish. There was nothing very encouraging in being described as sensible. In her own mind she acknowledged that it would be of equal benefit to her to have Lavender's companionship. The girl's quiet but intelligent presence was proving a good antidote to Julia's petty demands and spiteful asides. She could scarcely express such a view to Lewis, however, particularly given that he seemed to view Julia as the perfection of womanhood.

The gig trundled down the hill towards the village. Caroline watched Lewis's hands on the reins, tanned and strong, and repressed a shiver. She would be glad to be out of such close proximity. There was something about him that disturbed her equilibrium, and Caroline was unaccustomed at having to deal with such inappropriate feelings.

They clattered up the cobbled street and into the Manor courtyard. A groom came out to take the reins whilst Lewis jumped down and offered a hand to help

Caroline descend. 'It seems to me, ma'am,' he said slowly, 'that we started our conversation talking of *your* tastes and preferences, and swiftly moved to discussing everything from my view of the estate to my sister's accomplishments! Are you always so adroit at turning the conversation?'

Caroline blushed and tried to withdraw her hand from his grasp, but he did not release her. She thought fleetingly that it was odd that no one else had ever noticed how she tried to efface herself, but then that was probably a measure of her success. Most people who knew her would probably concur that Miss Whiston was good at her job, a little severe perhaps, but that was only to be expected in a governess companion. Of her interests and pastimes they would have no knowledge and express no interest. That was how she had always wanted it to be—until now. She looked into Lewis Brabant's blue eyes, softening now with the smile that was creeping in, and felt a strange pang in her heart. For a moment she entertained the thought that this was a man with whom she would gladly share her ideas, her interests. She dismissed the idea a second later, for it was foolish, painful and, she acknowledged, utterly without future.

Chapter Four

That evening was the first time that Caroline had
dined with the family since Lewis's return, and the
contrast between her own grey worsted and Julia's
confection of silk and lace reminded her forcibly of
the difference in their circumstances. She felt a frump
in her plain grey dress, very much the companion,
paid to be seen and not heard, to fade effortlessly into
the background. Small wonder that Lewis could not
even see her when Julia was by. She knew she was
a fool to imagine that it could ever be any other way.

Such uncharacteristically diffident thoughts made
Caroline hesitate in the drawing-room doorway.
Lewis and Julia were sitting together before the fire,
apparently engrossed in an animated debate about the
decoration of the house. The lamplight gleamed on
Julia's golden curls and sparkling blue eyes. She
looked both elegant and appealingly fragile, and
Caroline thought drily that Lewis seemed utterly cap-
tivated.

'...Red damask and rose wood,' Julia was saying

in her languid drawl. 'You must let me have the re-
furbishment of this room, Lewis! It could be so
Tonnish…'

'My dear Julia,' Lewis said wryly, 'it will be several years before I can even think of restoring the
house! There are fences to be mended and walls to
be rebuilt so that my father's tenants may prosper in
their business—'

'Oh, pooh!' Julia sounded almost petulant. 'Why
must they come first? You *must* decorate the house,
Lewis! No one will call if they think they are visiting
a mausoleum! Why—' She broke off as she saw
Caroline hovering in the doorway. 'Caro! So you
have finally succumbed to my invitations and decided
to join us for dinner!'

Caroline fought down a prickle of annoyance. For
Julia to imply that she had pressed invitations upon
her was bad enough, but then to be addressed as Caro,
in a pretence of friendship, was too much. She came
forward smiling a little stiffly and already regretting
the impulse that had led her to agree to dine with
them. Lewis rose to his feet politely at her approach
and sketched a bow. Caroline, contrasting his cool
courtesy with the warmth she had just seen him show
Julia, felt a sudden pang of desolation.

'A glass of wine, Miss Whiston?' Lewis asked, 'or
some ratafia, perhaps? It will only be a few minutes
until we dine.'

Caroline accepted a glass of wine and went across
to the window seat, where Lavender was reading a
book and making no pretence of joining in the general

conversation. This segregation seemed to suit Julia, who had already taken up again the theme of restoring the estate at the price of neglecting the house. She was leaning towards Lewis and touching his hand lightly to emphasise some point she was making. Caroline looked away deliberately and was glad when Lavender gave her a warm smile and gestured to her to sit down.

'Good evening, Caroline! It is pleasant to have some alternative company!' There was a spark of humour in Lavender's voice. 'I fear that I have little of use to add to Cousin Julia's discussions on household furnishings!'

They fell to talking about Lavender's book, which was Mary Elizabeth Jackson's *Botanical Dialogues*, until the gong sounded. Lewis gave Julia his arm into the dining-room and Caroline and Lavender followed behind.

Caroline privately thought that the cook had excelled herself with the dinner, but Julia was less impressed and compared the dishes unfavourably with the sort of meals she had experienced in London.

'The banquets were so lavish!' she observed. 'So elegant! Why, I recall an occasion when the dear Prince Regent had served forty-eight dishes in one evening!'

'Enough to bring on a fit of indigestion!' Lavender commented sweetly.

Julia fixed her with a cold blue gaze. Caroline waited to see if she would administer a set-down and concluded that it was only Lewis's presence that held her back.

'Do you remember the hideous meals we used to be given at Mrs Guarding's school, Caro?' Julia continued, shivering artistically. 'Boiled mutton and squab pie! It is a wonder I survived at all!'

Caroline thought that she heard Lavender murmur, 'And a pity!' but she could not be sure.

She applied herself to her food. It seemed safer to say nothing, and as far as she was concerned the meal could not be over soon enough. She had no intention of being used as a foil by Julia, who obviously wished to dominate the conversation with her sparkling wit.

Lavender also bent her head over her plate and did not speak again. Watching her face, Caroline wondered suddenly how Lavender must have felt when Julia invaded her home again. It seemed unlikely that Julia had even stopped to consider Lavender's feelings, and since she made no secret of her rather condescending pity for the girl, Caroline could hardly wonder at Lavender's dislike. Once again, Julia reminded her of the cuckoo in the Hewly nest.

She looked up, and saw that Lewis Brabant was watching his sister with a rather curious expression on his face. Caroline speculated that perhaps he was wondering how to smooth over the antipathy between Julia and Lavender. She was certain that he had already realised just how difficult it would make his life if his future wife and sister did not see eye to eye. Still, that would hardly be sufficient to discourage a determined man, and from what she knew of Captain

Brabant, Caroline suspected that he could be very single-minded in achieving his aims… She looked up to see that his gaze had transferred itself to her. For a moment it seemed that he had correctly divined her thoughts, for he raised an eyebrow in a quizzical gesture, and Caroline stared back transfixed before lowering her gaze again and trying to hide her blushes.

Dinner dragged on. It was one of the most uncomfortable meals that Caroline could remember. She positively jumped up from the table when it was time for the ladies to withdraw and leave Lewis to his solitary port. They retired to the drawing-room and Julia immediately began a patronising attack on Lavender's choice of pale blue for an evening gown. It was evident to Caroline that Julia had only been waiting her opportunity.

'That colour makes you look so pasty, my dear Lavender—so sallow! Not that any colour is likely to flatter, for your complexion is so washed-out! Perhaps a cerise…' Julia put her head on one side thoughtfully. 'No, that would be too strong…or yellow—'

'I like the blue,' Lavender said, in a tight little voice.

Julia laughed lightly. 'Yes, my dear, but what do you really know of matters of style? It does not surprise me that you could not catch yourself a husband when you were in London! Why, most of the gentlemen probably scarce noticed you were there!'

The colour rushed into Lavender's face. 'We are not all concerned with entrapping a husband, cousin Julia! I would as lief catch a cold!'

'Well, but you cannot expect to stay here for ever,' Julia said brightly, and it seemed to Caroline, an embarrassed observer, that she had reached the real point of what she was saying. 'Your brother will marry and will scarce wish his little sister to be hanging about the house—'

Caroline cleared her throat, about to intervene to try to pacify the situation, when the door opened and Lewis strolled in. He took in Lavender's angry face, Julia's smug one and Caroline's strained expression, and raised his eyebrows expressively. Caroline was glad to see him so soon, for his presence could not but ease the situation. On the other hand she was surprised; if she had been in his position she would have taken refuge in the study and finished the whole bottle of port.

'Let us have a round of whist!' Julia exclaimed suddenly, clapping her hands. 'That would be just the thing to cheer us up! Lewis, will you partner me?' She gave him a melting smile. 'It will be so much more exciting if you do!'

Caroline studiously avoided looking at either Lewis or Lavender. Whist was not her interest, though she played competently enough, having been asked to make up the numbers on many occasions. It soon became clear that Julia had deliberately chosen a pastime at which she shone. She won handsomely, mainly through chattering all the time and distracting her opponents. After one round, Lavender excused herself and went to bed.

'Country hours! So dull!' Julia yawned. 'You must

take a house in Town, Lewis! The country is so dreadfully slow! The Percevals and Cleeves do not entertain...and as for Sywell! Well, it is shocking that he should be allowed to be the premier landowner in the neighbourhood when he positively ignores us all!'

Caroline saw Lewis smile. 'I am sure that invitations will be forthcoming soon, Julia! As for Sywell, I confess I would not wish to visit the Abbey even if he invited me!'

Julia shrugged gracefully. 'Oh well, the Marquis is a scandal, I suppose, but the others have no excuse! You must call on them, Lewis! I do not care to be ignored by half the county! I shall quite die of boredom if we do not go out and about a bit more!'

'You have no obligation to stay here if you are so tired of.our company, Julia!' Lewis said, moving over to the sideboard and pouring a glass of wine. Caroline thought she could detect the tiniest hint of laughter in his voice. 'If you would prefer to leave us for the social delights of the Little Season—'

'Oh, I shall stay!' Julia said hastily. 'You know how concerned I am to see that dear Uncle Harley is cared for! Besides, it will soon be Christmas and I am sure we shall be as merry as grigs!'

Lewis frowned slightly. 'Father's illness must inevitably curtail our celebrations, I fear. A quiet, family Christmas—'

Caroline saw Julia frown briefly. 'But there is the ball at the Angel in a few weeks! Surely you would not seek to curb our pleasure so severely?' She gave him a reproachful glance. 'Why, Lewis, you are the veriest puritan!'

Caroline got to her feet. The prospect of watching Julia exert her charm was not a tempting one and she had been wishing to retire for the past two hours anyway. She felt a very unwelcome third, and Julia had been looking daggers at her in an unsubtle attempt to hint her away.

'If you will excuse me,' she murmured, 'I believe I shall retire now.'

'Oh, you may go!' Julia waved a hand in lordly dismissal. 'But pray do not lag abed in the morning, Caroline, for I have some commissions for you!'

Caroline smarted with annoyance at the implication that she was lazy and closed her lips tightly to prevent a sharp rejoinder from escaping. She swept out into the hall and was somewhat surprised to find that Lewis had followed her to light a candle for her.

'Thank you for your company this evening, Miss Whiston,' he said politely. 'I hope that you did not find it too much of a trial!'

Caroline met his eyes, which held a distinctly speculative twinkle deep in the blue. She was not sure of his precise meaning and did not intend to pursue it. The honest reply was that she would rather pull her hair out with tweezers than endure another dinner in Julia's company, but that would scarcely be diplomatic. She could not resist a look into the drawing-room, where Julia was drumming her fingers discontentedly on the arm of her chair. The Beauty's mouth drooped petulantly and she darted a sharp glance out into the hall, no doubt resenting that she was no longer the centre of Lewis's attention.

'It was a pleasant enough evening, but I would not wish to intrude on a family event again!' Caroline said neatly, taking the candlestick and evading Lewis's observant gaze. 'Good night, sir!'

She could not be sure, but she thought she heard him laugh as she sped up the stairs. When she reached the landing, however, the drawing-room door was just closing, affording a golden glimpse of Julia, now wreathed in smiles. Lewis was bending close to her, touching his glass to hers in a toast. Then the door shut, leaving Caroline out in the dark.

December, 1811

The month of December crept in with a return to hard frosts and cold blue skies. Julia's mood was poor and she vented her spleen on Caroline. Lady Perceval's promised invitation had arrived and, just as Caroline had expected, it was pointedly addressed to Lewis and Lavender only.

'The wretched woman knows full well that I am living here too!' Julia screeched, throwing her silver hairbrush across the room so that it bounced off the door panels. 'I would hardly expect her to invite you, Caroline, but why should I be excluded, pray? And as for Lewis—' her matching silver comb followed the brush '—he has gone out shooting with a party from Jaffrey House! It isn't fair! They have always been too high in the instep to acknowledge me, whilst

Lavender—' She broke off, almost choking with rage. 'That little nonentity—'

'Pray be calm, Julia,' Caroline said, retrieving the hairbrush. She had already resolved that the only way to sooth Julia was to treat her as she would a child having a tantrum. 'Such passion will make you ill! Take several deep breaths and quieten down!'

Julia glared at her. 'Calm! Why should I be calm? Just because my father made his fortune in trade— why, he could have bought them up ten times over! And who are the Brabants, after all? The Admiral was only a younger son, and his wife had no money! Yet they are invited everywhere whilst I am left to rot!'

Caroline itched to slap her, but reluctantly abandoned the thought. Nor would the truth help at this stage, for it contained the hard fact that Julia was more snobbish than any of her neighbours and was unwelcome more because of her manners than her background.

'Perhaps the Percevals thought that you would not be staying long,' she said soothingly, 'and besides, the situation may work to your benefit in the end.'

Julia stared at her suspiciously. 'What can you mean, Caroline? What possible benefit could there be in being ignored by one of the premier families in the neighbourhood?'

Caroline continued to fold Julia's clothes and put them into the chest of drawers. Julia had thrown them all over the floor earlier in her tantrum. 'Only that if the Captain and Miss Brabant go to dine at Perceval Hall, they will be sure to invite the family here to

Hewly in return, and the Percevals may not refuse!'
She looked up to see Julia watching her with a calculating look in her eyes. 'That will be your opportunity to act as hostess!'

'As long as that foolish little whey-faced sister of
Lewis's does not think to act the lady of the manor
herself!' Julia said viciously. 'Lewis had rather ask a
milk-churn to host the Percevals than ask Lavender!'

Caroline winced. The more friendly she became
with Lavender, the more difficult it was to bear Julia's
criticism of her, and Caroline was uncomfortably
aware that Lavender Brabant was worth a hundred
Julia Chessfords. Not for the first time, Caroline reflected that she should start to look for another position. She had been at Hewly for barely three months,
but her difficulties with Julia had already convinced
her that a long stay was out of the question. It was
not easy to find a suitable position of course, and it
might take her some time, which was all the more
reason to start at once. There had been Lady
Perceval's kind offer, but that would mean admitting
that there were problems at Hewly Manor and
Caroline shrank from exposing that to the outside
world. Gossip in the villages was bad enough as it
was, with everyone knowing each other's business, or
making it up if they did not. She did not imagine that
Lady Perceval herself would gossip, but word would
get out. It always did.

There was still Lady Covingham, the mother of her
previous charges. She might know of someone in
need of a governess. Caroline sighed silently. Anne

Covingham had been so delighted that Caroline was going to be companion to an old friend that it would be disappointing to have to admit that matters had not worked out. Still, beggars could not be choosers. Caroline resolved to write that day.

'I hear that Lewis has invited a friend to visit,' Julia was saying, preening before the mirror now that her good humour was restored. 'Captain Slater, with whom Lewis stayed when he was first ashore. Apparently the Captain was invalided out of the Navy a few years back and has a house in Lyme Regis— small fry to Lewis's fortune, but he might do for you, I suppose, Caroline!'

Caroline flushed. 'Thank you, Julia, but I am not intending to set my cap at Captain Brabant's friends!'

Julia shrugged carelessly. 'Pon rep, you are very haughty today! Well, I shall not throw him in your way if you do not wish to try your luck!' Her sharp gaze appraised Caroline thoughtfully. 'I suppose there is always Mr Grizel if you prefer a parson! Now, pray send Letty to me. She is to fit my new dresses!'

Caroline left the room feeling very short-tempered. She went first to the library and composed a letter to Lady Covingham, enquiring carefully over the possibility of employment. Then, still feeling irritated, she donned a warm cloak and stout shoes, and went out into the garden, hoping that the fresh air would soothe her annoyance. It was a cold day but the fresh chill of the air was bracing.

The kitchen gardens at Hewly were still tended, and provided fruit and vegetables for both the household and the village, but the Admiral's gardener had been unable to keep up the flower gardens without any additional help and had reluctantly let these run wild. As far as Caroline could ascertain, it was not a want of money that had led to the neglect of Hewly Manor, but rather the lack of a firm hand on the tiller for the last few years. The servants had high hopes that Lewis would now provide that guidance, and Caroline thought that they were probably correct. She knew they all had high hopes of the Captain and could not believe that these would be dashed. Not unless Lewis chose to sell the estate in time and return to sea... Caroline grimaced. That would be viewed as a sad event in the servants' hall, but perhaps not so bad as were Julia to become mistress...

Stifling such disloyal thoughts, Caroline walked briskly past the vegetable beds and into the flower gardens. Now that winter was approaching, she was able to trace the lines of the old garden beneath the weeds and tumbledown walls. Here was the rose walk, the bushes in dire need of a hard pruning, and along the old stone walls were the woody stems of lavender. A faint hint of their scent still hung in the air, taking Caroline back to her youth. She could see her grandmother, a huge apron over her old clothes as she collected sprigs of lavender in the gardens at Watchbell Hall. The tiny scented bags would be placed among the crisp sheets in the linen cupboards and Caroline would go to sleep breathing their perfume.

She had a sudden, painful pang of nostalgia, a

shocking wrench of homesickness that took her completely by surprise. Over the years, Caroline had seldom allowed herself to feel sorry that she had no home of her own, but now her loss suddenly overwhelmed her. She felt as small and lonely as a child.

She blinked back the tears and hurried out of the rose garden, almost tripping over the fallen sundial in her rush to escape her memories. She had no real notion where she was going, but she turned sharply into the topiary walk, where the flagged path gave way to a grassy avenue of yew. Rounding a corner, she collided with a figure standing in the shadow of one of the huge trees. Strong arms immediately encircled her, setting her back on her feet. She swayed a little and the arms tightened, steadying her.

'Miss Whiston?' Lewis's voice was close in her ear. 'Are you quite well, ma'am?'

Being so close to Lewis again felt both disturbingly familiar and confusing to Caroline's already troubled mind. She pulled back sharply.

'I beg your pardon, sir. I...' Caroline broke off. Her voice was still shaky with tears and for a moment she was afraid that it would desert her completely. Worse, she now realised that Lewis was not alone, for Belton, the gardener, was close by and he and Lewis had evidently been consulting over the need to cut the yews down to their original size. A stepladder was propped against the hedge and various gardening tools lay scattered across the path. Feeling foolish, Caroline tried to walk past, but Lewis stayed her by the simple expedient of keeping hold of her arm.

'A moment, Miss Whiston! It is fortunate that you passed this way, for I wonder if you could spare me a little of your time?' He turned to the gardener. 'Thank you very much, Belton. We will talk on this again soon.'

The gardener touched his cap and nodded to Caroline before moving off in an unhurried manner towards his greenhouses. Once he was out of sight, Caroline turned to Lewis and pointedly pulled her arm from his grip.

'What do you mean by restraining me thus, sir? And in front of your servants! I intended to walk by—' Her words came out with more sharpness than she had intended and she stopped, realising that her recent distress was still close to the surface. She had the disturbing feeling that Lewis, whose eyes were moving slowly over her face, was also aware of the fact.

'I realise that,' he said gently. 'That was why I stopped you. I was concerned that there might be something wrong and thought that I might be able to help. You seem a little distraught, Miss Whiston.'

Caroline realised with dismay that her tears had dried on her cheeks, leaving tell-tale marks below her eyes. She felt confused by his perception and brushed them away self-consciously.

'It was nothing, sir. There is nothing the matter.'

Having rubbed her face, Caroline turned her attention to removing some stray leaves from her cloak. She did not look at him. There was a silence.

'I see,' Lewis said slowly. 'That would account for

your tears, of course. Well, if you do not wish to tell me I cannot force you to do so—'

'I was feeling foolishly nostalgic,' Caroline said in a rush, 'and I fear I was not looking where I was going. Pray do not let me take you from your work, sir.'

'Perhaps you might accompany me,' Lewis suggested quietly. 'I am planning improvements to the gardens, as you see, and would appreciate your advice. Will you help?'

Caroline found herself taking his arm and walking slowly down the grassy path. She was not entirely sure how she had come to accept Lewis's suggestion, for her first instinct had been to flee from him. Now, however, he was talking of his plans and she was soon distracted.

'I am hoping that we might eventually re-create the gardens that were here when Hewly was part of the Perceval estate,' Lewis was saying, holding some trailing sprays of honeysuckle aside for Caroline to follow him into the first of the walled gardens. 'There are still designs of the ground plan in the Library. Belton's grandfather tended the gardens here in the early days of George III and he tells me that they were spoken of as very fine. There was a series of walled gardens here with fruit and cold frames, and any number of fine trees in the park. There is much work to do but I feel I must make a start.'

Caroline hesitated. She remembered Lavender saying that she was not sure if Lewis would even wish to stay at Hewly. It seemed strangely reassuring that he was planning a restoration project, for surely he would not trouble to do so if he intended to sell the estate. She looked about her carefully, at the old, tumbledown walls and the trailing strands of honeysuckle and rose. In the summer the walled gardens would be a charming sun-trap, but now they just looked neglected and lost.

'I imagine that such a scheme would take several years,' she said tentatively, 'though it would surely be worthwhile in the end.'

'Why, so I hope!' Lewis smiled at her. He was assessing the state of the masonry with an experienced eye. 'If I am to remain here at Hewly I intend to try to restore it to some of its former glory! Though whether I shall be able to create a lake to assuage my need for the sea, I am not so sure!'

Caroline laughed aloud. 'Perhaps you could design a lake, or at least a small pond! Is there not a stream that runs across the far side of the orchard? It drains into the river and I am sure you could dam it if you wished to emulate the work of garden designers of old!' She brushed her fingers against the wall. 'This seems sound enough, and I believe I have seen some statuary in these gardens too...' She pushed aside a huge clump of nettles with a gloved hand. 'Yes, here is one! I am sure that you will find that the foundations of the garden are still here under all the weeds...'

Lewis had come across to see the statue. It was of a stone cherub, curly-haired and with an innocently saucy tilt to its head. Lewis leant over and Caroline

was suddenly sharply aware of his nearness. The wind
was ruffling his thick fair hair and he pushed it back
from his eyes with an impatient hand. The hard lines
of his cheek and jaw were so close that she had to
prevent herself from reaching out to trace them with
her fingers. He touched the cherub's head lightly and
Caroline was shocked to feel the echo of that touch
through her own body. She turned away abruptly,
afraid that her face would betray her.

Suddenly the cold day seemed as bright and hot as
high summer. With heightened awareness, Caroline
knew that Lewis was watching her and had sensed
her feelings. She caught a stem of honeysuckle between her fingers and cast desperately around for
some topic to lessen the tension.

'This is growing wild now, but Belton could soon
clip it back into shape—'

Lewis' fingers covered hers on the stem. She could
feel the warmth of his touch through her gloves and
fell silent. Then his hand came up and brushed a stray
strand of hair back from her face.

'Keep still.' His voice was husky. 'You have a briar
rose caught in your hair…' He untangled it deftly, the
touch of his fingers against her skin making Caroline
shiver. She stepped back abruptly and almost fell over
a low wall.

'I must go now,' she said, knowing she sounded
breathless. Her heart was beating fast and she could
not look at Lewis. 'Mrs Chessford…she is having her
dresses fitted…she may need me…'

It was as though the mention of Julia's name

caused some kind of constraint between them. Lewis stepped back, his expression unreadable, and Caroline shot through the door in the wall as though the hounds of Hades were at her heels. She turned towards the house, hoping desperately that Lewis would not follow her. She needed some time to calm herself.

'Slow down, or you may trip again,' Lewis caught up with her as she reached the yew walk. He spoke in impersonal tones and when Caroline glanced at his face she saw with relief that it was quite expressionless. That extraordinary moment in the walled garden might never have occurred. Only the slight trembling of her hands betrayed the fact that it had.

'You mentioned feeling nostalgic, Miss Whiston,' Lewis said, after a moment. 'Tell me, where was your home originally?'

'Oh…' Caroline rallied herself to speak normally. She slowed her pace, aware that she was becoming out of breath. 'My family were from Cumbria, sir.'

'The Whistons of Watchbell Hall?' Lewis put his hands in his pockets. 'I had no idea that you were related to that family. Was your grandfather not a famous collector of clocks and watches, playing on the name of his home? I am sure I heard that he had some of John Harrison's original timepieces?'

Caroline smiled. 'He did indeed. I have one of them as a keepsake—only small, but very dear to me.'

Lewis squared his shoulders. 'Forgive me if I speak out of turn, Miss Whiston, but did you not have any relatives who might help you upon your father's death? It seems most singular that you had to go out and earn a living!'

'A distant cousin of my father's inherited the title.' Caroline met his eyes a little defiantly. 'I had no wish to be a burden on a family I barely knew. I make shift as well I can.'

'I imagine so. You seem most resourceful, Miss Whiston, but—' Lewis broke off. 'Forgive me,' he said again, 'it is none of my concern after all.'

A slightly strained silence fell between them. Caroline was profoundly grateful that they were nearly back on the terrace now. The mossy stones were smooth beneath her feet and, mindful of the first day she had met Lewis, she was careful not to slip.

'Perhaps you might help me with my garden plan if you have the time,' Lewis continued, on a lighter note. 'I know that Belton respects your opinion. He mentioned that you had given him advice on treatment for some of the diseased roses!'

Caroline smiled. 'I am happy to help if Mrs Chessford can spare me,' she said. 'Whilst I am at Hewly I should like to be useful.'

Lewis tilted his head. 'It sounds as though you do not intend to be with us much longer, Miss Whiston,' he said acutely. 'Are you thinking of leaving?'

Caroline looked away. She knew she should have been more careful, for she was already aware of Lewis's sometimes uncanny perception.

'I have no other plans at present,' she said truthfully. 'Good day, sir.'

She slipped inside and closed the door behind her,

resisting the impulse to watch Lewis as he strolled off in the direction of Belton and the greenhouses. It seemed that she had vastly underestimated the case when she had imagined that she should be able to avoid the Captain. What she had not underestimated, however, was the need to do so. After eleven years as a governess in households up and down the country, she was in danger of succumbing to the sort of feelings she had never experienced for any man. It was dangerous, inappropriate and all the things that Miss Caroline Whiston was not. It also emphasised the need to leave Hewly before her feelings made a complete fool of her. She would do best to leave the garden lost in time, and her own feelings frozen with it.

The Admiral's condition worsened the following day and an exhausted Mrs Prior gladly accepted Caroline's offer to sit with him for a few hours whilst she tried to get some rest. The doctor had called earlier and had confided that he thought that the end was very near, a few weeks at the most. Word had got around the house, with the effect that unhappiness sat like a pall over the place. The servants whispered and tiptoed about, Lavender moped in the library and Julia was even more irritable than usual.

'I do not see why Lewis feels we must all creep about like ghosts!' she said crossly to Caroline. 'Much more of this and we shall *all* expire—from boredom, if nothing else!' She flounced across her bedroom. 'I did not imagine that this would happen so soon! If Uncle Harley dies there will be no more parties and no entertainment and then where shall we be! We shall not even be able to attend the Christmas ball at the Angel!'

'I am sure that the Admiral will take that into account when he plans just when to pass away!' Caroline said, for once not trying to conciliate her friend. Julia's blue eyes widened to their furthest extent.

'Why, you are very cross today! What is it to you that Admiral Brabant is about to die? *You* cannot share our distress!'

Caroline held on to her temper with an effort. 'I am naturally upset by such an event,' she said evenly. 'It is true that I do not know the Admiral well, but I can still regret his illness! Why, the servants are all worried, and Miss Brabant is deeply upset—'

'Oh, Lavender!' Julia sniffed. 'Well, I suppose that is not be wondered at! I shall do my best to comfort her, of course, but it is Lewis that I worry over, coming home to all this! I feel I must devote myself to ensuring his future happiness!'

'I am sure that he will be most grateful to you!' Caroline snapped. 'Excuse me, I do not believe I can do anything more here, so I shall go downstairs!'

Julia raised her brows. 'Very well! I shall come down too and play the piano! Some music may banish the blue devils in me!'

Once Julia was settled in the music room, Caroline went to see if she could find Lavender.

The December afternoon was dark already, as

though echoing the sombre mood in the house. Lavender was not in the Library or the drawing-room, and Caroline was about to enquire if any of the servants knew of her whereabouts, when the study door opened and Lewis Brabant came out. He looked cross and harassed, and Caroline gave him a tentative smile, aware that he must be feeling as dismal as his sister. It evoked no answering gleam. To the contrary, there was a hard light in Lewis's blue eyes as they dwelled on her and a harsh set to his mouth. Caroline's heart did a little nervous jump.

'Miss Whiston.' Lewis's tone was clipped. 'How convenient. I wonder if you would spare me a moment of your time, ma'am?'

'Of course—' Caroline frowned a little, taken aback. She could think of nothing she had done that would merit the look of dislike in Lewis's eyes. She felt like a recalcitrant lieutenant who was about to be hauled over the coals.

Her apprehension rose as he ushered her into the study and closed the door very firmly behind them. He did not invite her to sit down; he himself walked over to the window and stared out over the darkened garden for a few moments before swinging round on her.

'Can you tell me what this is, Miss Whiston?'

Caroline followed his gaze, feeling utterly bewildered. He had thrown something down on the blotter of his desk and Caroline stepped forward to try to see what it was that he was talking about. It looked like a letter, the paper faded, the writing extravagant with loops and curls. Caroline suddenly recognised it as one of Julia's letters from years before, and frowned as she tried to imagine how it could have fallen into Lewis's hands.

'Why, yes… It is an old letter from Mrs Chessford to myself, but—'

'Do you keep all your old letters, Miss Whiston?' Lewis interrupted her with scant courtesy. 'It seems a somewhat singular thing to do!' He drove his hands into his pockets as though to restrain himself from some more violent action. Once again his gaze raked her with dislike. 'Unless, of course, you have some purpose in mind for them!'

Caroline looked at him in bewilderment. 'I kept Julia's letters only because they reminded me of my time at school here. They were a link with my childhood. But I do not understand… How did you gain possession of this, sir?'

Lewis gave her a scathing look and at the same moment, Caroline remembered. Her hand flew to her mouth as she realised that she must have accidentally left the letter in the book of poetry she had taken down to the library. She had been reading *Marmion* one evening when Mrs Prior had come to ask for her assistance with the Admiral, and she had pushed the letter carelessly inside it to keep her place. Later she had taken the book up again and put her bookmark absentmindedly inside the front cover. So the letter must still have been there when she had returned the book, and Lewis had picked it up himself with some remark about enjoying the work…

Caroline caught her breath, wondering which of Julia's indiscreet observations were recorded in that particular letter. How much of it had Lewis read? There must be something in it, to make him react so. Was it the one about Julia's engagement to Andrew Brabant, or was there some reflection on Lewis himself…?

Caroline became aware of Lewis watching her with a penetrating regard. His scrutiny was thorough, from head to foot, and there was a frown between his eyes.

'Oh dear… I am so sorry…' She stopped. Too late, she realised that Lewis had interpreted her words as some kind of admission of guilt, for he was smiling grimly.

'I confess myself disappointed that you should stoop to so clumsy a piece of subterfuge, Miss Whiston,' he said coldly. 'To conceal a letter in the book is an old ruse and one that can only be designed to stir up trouble! What was your aim? To provoke discord between Mrs Chessford and myself! I had thought better of you, ma'am, but now I think it wise for you to start your packing! You will leave Hewly Manor immediately!'

Chapter Five

Caroline stared at Lewis in fury. She was almost breathless with shock and outrage. The suddenness of her dismissal was almost too much to take in.

'Leave Hewly? How dare you make such a presumption of guilt, sir! And you are not my employer, sir, to dismiss me on a whim!'

'But it is my house!' Lewis leant both hands on the desk and returned Caroline's furious regard with a gaze that was equally angry. 'Therefore I say that you should go!'

'In point of fact, sir,' Caroline said evenly, 'it is *not* your house and I am sure that your father would never behave in so arrogant and high-handed a manner!'

Lewis took a deep breath. He straightened up. 'Leaving aside your aspersions on my behaviour, Miss Whiston, do I take it that you deny you played such a trick?'

Caroline spoke cuttingly. 'I beg your pardon, sir. I fear I do not even understand this farrago of nonsense! Do *you* imply that I left the letter in the book deliberately?'

Lewis looked at her in silence. His anger seemed to have gone and Caroline could discern nothing in his face but resignation and a fleeting disappointment. For some reason this made her even more furious. He made a slight gesture with his hands.

'What else am I to think, Miss Whiston? It appears that you left a damaging letter specifically for me to find! No doubt you hoped I should read it, and that its childish revelations would injure the regard I have for Mrs Chessford! I would not have thought you capable of such a deceit were it not for what Mrs Chessford herself had mentioned to me this afternoon—' He broke off, but Caroline was too quick for him.

'Indeed, sir? Pray do not scruple to tell me! After such an injury as you have already dealt me, further accusations can be as nothing!'

Lewis looked slightly uncomfortable. 'Miss Whiston—'

Caroline was not about to let him retreat. 'Captain Brabant? I am waiting!'

Lewis sat down. It was a disarming move and left Caroline feeling slightly foolish that she was still standing in so rigid a pose. When he gestured to her to take the chair opposite, she had little alternative but to comply.

'Miss Whiston,' Lewis said slowly, 'perhaps it is better that we set this aside as a misunderstanding—'

He got no further. Caroline was still furious and

she suspected that he was only trying to protect Julia. She leant forward threateningly, her hazel eyes flashing.

'Captain Brabant! If you do not tell me at once what it was that Julia said—'

'You will do what, Miss Whiston?' Lewis met her gaze coolly, calling her bluff. A slight smile touched the corners of his mouth. 'Can you not accept that there has been a mistake—'

'Oh, fustian! Do not seek to gammon me, sir!' Caroline gave him a look of disgust. 'I suppose that Julia said that I had left my last post under a cloud or that I had been turned off…' She saw by the way his eyes narrowed that she had hit her mark. 'And you believed her!' Caroline added sharply. 'You have made some fine assumptions, have you not, sir, believing that I have a penchant for malicious tricks and that Julia only employs me through kindness since I am so deceitful!'

She locked her hands together to still their shaking. 'I freely admit to leaving the letter in the poetry book, but I did so in all innocence. If you will recall,' she glared at him across the space between them, 'it was *your* idea to borrow *Marmion* and no suggestion of mine! I could not have contrived such a trick even had I wished! It was the veriest accident!'

Their gazes locked, Lewis's watchful, Caroline's bright with anger and distress. 'As for this other tale,' she continued, 'the one of my apparent untrustworthiness—*that* is the fabrication, not my behaviour! I have references, couched in the highest terms, but since Mrs Chessford evidently believes me unreliable, I will leave her service at once! Leave Hewly? You would have to beg me to stay!'

She saw a flicker of a smile cross Lewis's face. There was a very definite admiration in his eyes now, admiration and something even more disquieting. Caroline jumped to her feet and made for the door. Lewis moved quickly to block her path.

'Miss Whiston! Wait!'

Caroline was already reaching for the handle when Lewis put a hand against the door panels and leant his weight on it to hold it closed. They were very close. Caroline stepped back, his proximity sending a sudden quiver of awareness through her. All her nerve endings seemed to be sensitised by their quarrel, her feelings too close to the surface. Some colour came into her set face. She kept her expression stony and avoided his eyes.

'You would prevent my departure now, sir? By what right—'

'Miss Whiston, do not run away!' Lewis spoke urgently, his gaze compelling on her face. 'Allow me to explain—'

'At your command, sir?' Caroline asked icily, covering her trembling with haughtiness.

Lewis straightened up. He raised an eyebrow. 'At my most humble prayer? Please, Miss Whiston, sit down again and hear me out…'

Caroline could feel herself weakening. She looked pointedly at him until he took his hand from the door.

'Please,' he said again. 'I should be grateful for the chance to put matters right, Miss Whiston…'

Caroline felt trapped. Good manners obliged her to do as he asked, although she had a most ardent wish to escape his presence. She waited as Lewis poured two glasses of madeira, sat down opposite her and put his own glass down on the small table between them. He looked at her thoughtfully.

'First, I believe I owe you an apology, ma'am.' There was a frown between his brows again. 'That was devilish clumsy of me, regardless of what I believed at the time. You were quite right to ring a peal over me for my bad manners. It was only because I felt so surprised—' He broke off abruptly. 'But that is nothing to the purpose.' His expression lightened a little. 'I believe this is no more than a misunderstanding and soon mended. I accept that you never meant to leave the letter in the book and certainly did not intend it for me.'

Caroline gave him a very straight look. 'Besides, what would be the point of such an action, sir? As a gentleman I know that you would never have read a letter addressed to another!'

There was a pause.

'As you say, ma'am.' Caroline thought she could see a glint of amusement in Lewis's eyes. 'I did in fact read a little of the letter in order to ascertain to whom it belonged—'

'Since they are all addressed to "dear Caro",' Caroline said acidly, 'that should not have taxed your intellect a great deal, sir!' She looked across to the desk, where the offending letter still rested on the leather top.

'Dear Caro…' Lewis said musingly, and there was a caressing tone in his voice that brought the colour into Caroline's cheeks. 'You are right, that was the appellation, and very pretty I thought it too…'

'That is beside the point, sir!' Caroline snapped, hoping that he put her blush down to anger not embarrassment. 'The issue here is that you apparently believed me capable of wishing to discredit Mrs Chessford! Worse, I believe you indicated that Mrs Chessford herself had some concerns over my integrity—'

'I must stress that this is all a misunderstanding on my part,' Lewis said smoothly, leaving Caroline almost speechless at the skilful way he was glossing over the situation. 'I must beg you to forgive me for a poor, dull fellow. Julia never implied such a thing, I am sure, and your integrity is unimpeachable, Miss Whiston…'

'But…' Caroline felt as though the rug had been pulled from beneath her. 'That is all very well, sir—'

Lewis shrugged casually. 'I would not wish this matter to cause trouble between you and Mrs Chessford, still less that you would feel it necessary to leave Hewly. Please forgive me for this storm in a teacup, my dear Miss Whiston, and accept another glass of wine as a peace offering!'

Caroline looked down and realised that she had already finished the first glass. She had no recollection of drinking it. She frowned a little, still thinking on what Lewis had just said.

'I cannot imagine,' she blurted out, 'why you should think I would wish to discredit Julia! What possible motive—' She broke off as Lewis turned to look at her, one brow raised quizzically.

'Oh no, Captain Brabant! I fear that you flatter yourself far too much!'

Lewis had the grace to look a little abashed. 'Miss Whiston, I was not really such a coxcomb as to believe that you had a partiality for me—'

'No, I dare say that Mrs Chessford planted that particular idea in your head as well!' Caroline's wrath was growing again, fuelled by the fact that there was more than a grain of truth in the idea. 'Of all the conceited... Have you forgotten, sir, that you were the one who forced your attentions on me when we first met! You do not see me begging for your notice!'

Lewis laughed. 'I most certainly have not forgotten...' He put the decanter down and came towards her. Caroline took one look at his face and felt suddenly breathless. Perhaps it had not been such a good idea to remind him of their encounter in the wood. She got clumsily to her feet.

'I believe I should go now, sir—'

'Must you? I felt sure we were about to have a most interesting debate—'

Caroline felt hot all over. It could have been the wine, or the heat from the fire, but she knew it was more likely to be her own unruly emotions. She moved towards the door, almost stumbling over the

hem of her dress in her haste to be away from him.
Lewis took her elbow to steady her and Caroline
snatched it away.

'Thank you, sir, I am able to manage very well!'

Caroline heard him laugh.

'I see.' He was reaching for the doorhandle and she
was inexpressibly relieved to see him open it this
time. 'And you will not leave Hewly over this unfortunate misunderstanding?'

Caroline bit her lip, suddenly sobering. Whatever
he said, the experience had soured her already equivocal friendship with Julia. She did not doubt that Julia
had cast aspersions on her integrity, and Lewis's
smooth pretence of a misunderstanding was just
that—a pretence. It left a bitter taste in her mouth.
Julia had told malicious lies about her and Lewis had
believed them. Caroline had been intending to leave
Hewly anyway, but this only reinforced her intention
to do so as soon as possible.

Lewis had evidently read her answer in her face.
He closed the door again.

'Miss Whiston,' he said slowly, 'I must beg you to
stay with us, at least for a little.' He leant back against
the door, his gaze very sombre. 'This is a bad time
for us. I have already observed that my sister has
started to rely on you as a friend and I believe she is
going to need that companionship very soon. I appeal
to you—if you cannot stay because of Julia, stay a
little to help Lavender.'

Caroline sighed. She felt trapped by his words. She
had already thought of the implications of leaving

Lavender in a house where her father was about to die and her cousin was a silly, vain creature incapable of offering her the support she needed. True, she had her brother, but he would have so many matters to attend to after their father's death. A few weeks ago it would not have mattered to her; a few weeks ago she had not come to like and respect Lavender Brabant. But now…

'I know it is unfair of me to ask you,' Lewis said, smiling ruefully. 'Believe me, I only do it because I feel that it is so important for my sister. But if you truly believe that you cannot bear to stay—'

'No,' Caroline spoke quickly. 'I will stay—for Miss Brabant's sake, at least for a little while.'

'Thank you.' Lewis took her hand and pressed a kiss on it. 'I am truly grateful, Miss Whiston. And for the other—'

'Do not let us speak of it again, sir.' Caroline withdrew her hand quickly.

'If you wish.' For once Lewis seemed oddly at a loss. 'One thing I must say, though, Miss Whiston. I was very wrong to doubt you, and for that I am truly sorry—'

Caroline made a dismissive gesture. She did not wish to pursue the subject, for thinking of it would only make her realise how sore her heart was. She allowed Lewis to open the door for her and walked slowly upstairs, aware of his gaze following her progress. When she had finally gained the sanctuary of her own room she closed the door softly and sat down, dry-eyed, in the chair beside the bed.

She did not wish to stay at Hewly Manor. The oppressive nature of the atmosphere was depressing and, taken with the evidence of Julia's malice, it created an unpleasant feeling in the pit of her stomach. Yet she had promised Lewis that she would stay, at least for a little, and she would keep that promise. She opened her eyes and stared at the black sky visible in the square panes of the window. He had said that he wanted her to stay to befriend Lavender, and she had agreed on those terms. Yet now she found herself acknowledging that she wished he had asked her to stay for himself.

The approach of Christmas was heralded by few of the usual festivities. Lavender and Lewis drove around the tenant farms and cottages, delivering presents and Christmas good wishes, but the atmosphere was subdued and the shadow of Admiral Brabant's illness lay over everyone. When Julia mooted the idea of attending the ball at the Angel, Lavender declined to go and Caroline chose to stay at home to keep her company. She could think of little worse than watching Julia flirt with Lewis all night and sitting on the sidelines whilst she waited for him to notice her and remember to offer her a courtesy dance.

Julia returned in high good spirits and full of gossip.

'The talk in the village is all of betrothals and weddings!' she said at breakfast the day after, looking impossibly fresh in a dress of yellow muslin with a matching bandeau in her hair. 'Beatrice Roade is to marry Lord Ravensden tomorrow and if it wasn't for this wretched snow we could all attend! She has done very well for herself, for Ravensden is an excellent catch!' She stirred her chocolate. 'Really, it is extraordinary how well these girls do when they have no looks or portion! When India Rushford caught Lord Isham it was marvel enough, but Beatrice Roade is an odd, outspoken girl...' Her gaze dwelled on Lavender for an instant.

Caroline buttered a second piece of toast. 'Perhaps Lord Ravensden enjoys Miss Roade's company, Julia.'

Julia's eyes opened very wide. 'Lud, what a strange notion, Caroline! Do you not remember,' she gave a little feline smile, 'that when we were at school we used to say that about the plain girls! The only way they would get an offer would be from some gentleman who thought they had a pleasant personality!' She gave a peal of laughter. 'Of course, in those days you were quite a pretty girl yourself—'

Lewis rustled his newspaper irritably. 'You have forgotten Viscount Wyndham, Julia! Do you not have some comment to make about him?'

'Why yes!' Julia seemed to completely miss Lewis's sarcasm, and turned to the others with sparkling eyes. 'The most piquant piece of gossip imaginable, my dears! They say that he sometimes has girls staying alone with him at his hunting-lodge near here—'

Lavender got up and very deliberately left the room. Julia stared.

'Well, upon my word—'

Lewis folded his newspaper, tucked it under his arm and rose to his feet. 'Excuse me. I shall be in the study if anyone requires me.'

Julia shrugged pettishly as the door closed behind him. 'What can be the matter with those two today? Now, did I tell you about Miss Reeth…'

Caroline sighed and poured herself another cup of chocolate. It seemed so unfair that she was the only one who could not simply get up and leave Julia to her own devices.

Admiral Brabant died three days after Christmas. It was hardly unexpected and all his family was with him at the end. Whilst they assembled at the bedside, Caroline took Nanny Prior down to the kitchens and poured her cup after cup of strong, sweet tea, listening sympathetically whilst she talked of her long association with the Brabant family and her sorrow that both the Admiral and his wife had now passed on. It was late in the evening and eventually Nanny Prior blew her nose hard on a capacious white handkerchief, gave Caroline a watery smile and said, 'Bless you for listening whilst I rambled on, child! It's a sad business, but I suppose there's always hope! When Master Lewis—the Captain, I should say, now that he's the head of the household—when he sets up his nursery, then we shall see brighter times ahead here at Hewly!'

Caroline stirred her tea and wondered whether Nanny Prior thought such an event was imminent.

'News of a betrothal might lift everyone's spirits,' Mrs Prior continued, obviously following the same train of thought herself. 'Though, I suppose, with the house in mourning…' She sighed. 'Then there's those who would not be so happy to see the match. Ah well, matters will resolve themselves in time! It's a sad homecoming for Miss Julia, though, with her uncle taken ill so soon after she arrived, and never in his senses again! Why, she was barely in the house two hours before he was struck down!'

Caroline could see quite easily how Nanny Prior had made the connection between Lewis's nuptials and Julia's presence at Hewly, and her heart sank. She could hardly ask the old nurse whether the servants thought a match between the two was a foregone con-clusion, and really Mrs Prior's comments spoke for themselves. With a sigh she helped herself to a piece of rich sponge cake, reflecting that eating for comfort was delicious but a bad idea, and that she would suf-fer for it when she finally came to try to sleep.

'We found him in the study with everything scat-tered about him,' Nanny Prior was continuing, with a certain gloomy relish. 'The ink pot had spilled all over the desk and the quill was on the floor—there were reams of paper everywhere! Proper mess it was, and with the Admiral lying insensible in the middle of it all! It's surprising the poor gentleman lasted as long as he did!'

'What was he writing?' Caroline asked, her mouth full of sponge cake.

Nanny Prior stared. She seemed much struck by the

question. 'Well! Now you're asking!' She frowned in perplexity. 'I don't rightly know, miss! Never thought on it again until now! There's a thing! A letter, I think it was, though so blotted and spotted you could hardly read…' She shook her head.

'Ah well.' Caroline drained her cup and wondered whether Lavender might need her. She was about to go upstairs to find out, when a maid stuck her head around the kitchen door, bobbed Mrs Prior the respectful curtsey of a junior to a senior servant, and addressed Caroline.

'Begging your pardon, ma'am, but Mrs Chessford is asking for you.'

Julia was waiting at the top of the stairs, weeping artistically into her lace handkerchief and leaning heavily on Lewis's arm.

'Caroline,' her former friend instructed as she wiped her eyes prettily, 'I require a hot posset to help me get what little sleep I can this wretched night. I *must* sleep, or I will look a hag in the morning.' She gave Lewis a sweet, mournful smile. 'Do you go down to the kitchens again and prepare a drink of milk and nutmeg for me, and Lewis, pray stay with me until Caro returns for I cannot bear to be left alone—' She broke off.

Lavender was coming out of the Admiral's bedchamber, her face pale and ravaged with tears. For a moment Caroline thought she saw a hint of chagrin in Julia's eyes, but the next moment she was drooping charmingly on Lewis's arm, murmuring that she felt a little faint. Caroline hurried across to put an arm around Lavender, calling to Lewis over her shoulder.

'Captain Brabant, I believe your sister needs you. I will assist Mrs Chessford to her room and fetch her a drink. Then, if I can be of any comfort to Miss Brabant—'

'Thank you, Miss Whiston.' Lewis dropped Julia's arm without a second glance, bestowed a grateful but distracted smile on Caroline, and crossed the landing to take Lavender in his arms. Caroline and Julia watched them walk away together, Lavender's fair head resting on his shoulder.

'Well!' Julia said, straightening up and suddenly sounding much stronger, 'you would have thought that Lewis would at least ascertain that I was quite well before he left me! I can scarce believe—'

'Julia,' Caroline said, in a voice of iron, 'Miss Brabant has just lost her father. Whilst I am sure that your feelings for your godfather were sincere, I do not believe that your loss can compare with hers. Now, I will go down to fetch you your drink, and I will send Letty up to attend you.'

Julia flounced off towards her room. 'You have become quite the managing creature, Caroline! Since nobody cares for me I shall do perfectly well on my own!'

Sighing, Caroline went back down to the kitchens. Cook was already there, stolidly stirring a pan of milk on the stove. She looked up and gave Caroline a faint smile.

'Miss Whiston, I've prepared some milk for my

little lamb and I'll slip a noggin of brandy in with some nutmeg so that she sleeps…'

For a moment, Caroline wondered whether Cook could be a lot more fond of Julia than she had always appeared to be, then she realised that the woman was talking about Lavender, not Julia.

'I will take Miss Brabant's drink up for her, if you wish,' she volunteered. 'I know you must all be at sixes and sevens down here…'

Cook threw her a grateful glance. 'Bless you, Miss Whiston, that we are! What with the housemaids crying in the pantry and John the footman gone to the village with the news and Nanny Prior awash with tea…'

'If there is any milk left, may I take it to Mrs Chessford?' Caroline asked carefully. 'I am sure she would be grateful for a cup—'

Cook sniffed. 'Grateful for nothing, that one! Complaining of us to the master, and queening it about the house as though she were mistress here already! Now the Honourable Mrs B., she was a proper lady. Turning in her grave she'll be to think of that one taking her place!'

Caroline realised that she had made a tactical error in raising Julia's name. She had known that most of the servants disliked Julia because she had complained to Lewis of their shoddy ways almost as soon as he was through the door. And Cook was obviously very upset at the Admiral's death, for she was wiping a surreptitious tear away with the corner of her apron and sniffing over the milk. Caroline patted her arm in a comforting manner and received a weak smile for her pains. Cook filled two cups with milk, handed the tray to Caroline and thanked her once again.

Caroline went upstairs and knocked on Julia's door. Letty answered and took the cup in, leaving Caroline relieved that she did not have to endure another of Julia's diatribes. Through the panels of the closed door she could hear Julia's voice rising and falling like a peal of bells. She went along the corridor, past a huddle of servants, and tapped on Lavender's bedroom door. She could hear a murmur of voices from within, and in a moment, Lewis Brabant opened the door.

'Miss Whiston,' he gave her a faint smile. 'Please come in.'

Caroline's heart ached for him. There were lines of exhaustion and grief on his face and his eyes were tired. She wanted to comfort him and take him in her arms, and the impulse was so strong that it shocked her. Fortunately, perhaps, she was still carrying the milk, and now a spot of the scalding liquid jumped from the cup on to her hand and recalled her to her senses. She carried the cup across to the bedside table and set it down carefully.

Lavender was sitting propped up on her pillows and she gave Caroline a pale smile. 'Thank you so much, Caroline. Will you sit with me for a little? Lewis has so many things that he must do.'

Caroline glanced questioningly at Lewis. He inclined his head slightly. 'If you would be so good, Miss Whiston.'

'Of course.' Caroline waited whilst Lewis bent down and kissed Lavender on the cheek, then she sat down at the side of the bed and took one of Lavender's hands in a comforting grasp.

'I am so sorry, Lavender. Although it was not sudden, it must still be a horrid shock for you.'

The younger girl gave her a grateful smile. 'Thank you, Caroline. Yes, it is hard. For all that I knew father was dying, it is difficult to believe that he is gone. Yet I am glad in a way, for he was not himself towards the end and now his suffering is over.'

She reached forward and Caroline passed her the cup of milk. 'Be careful, it is a little full.'

Lavender drank deeply. Her eyes were already closing when Caroline took the tilting cup from her hand and helped her to settle back on the pillows.

'Try to sleep, now. You are exhausted.'

'In a moment,' Lavender murmured. 'Caroline, do you think that Lewis will marry Julia?' Her eyes flickered open briefly, lavender blue and drowned with tears. 'Oh, I do so hope not! I could not bear it!'

Caroline was startled. It seemed to be the night when everybody's prejudices about Julia were coming to the fore. Either Cook had put too much brandy in the posset, or Lavender's grief had broken down the barriers of reticence, or perhaps both. She patted her hand.

'Do not worry about that now, Lavender.'

'No,' the girl turned her fair head against the pillow. 'Perhaps all will be well. It is just…' She hesitated, yawning. 'I do not like her, you see,' she said simply. 'Nor do I trust her. She was supposed to be marrying Lewis years ago, but as soon as he was gone to sea she threw him over for Andrew! Mama and papa did not like the match, but Julia made a dead set for him! She thought that I was too young to see what was happening, but I knew! It was only because Andrew was the elder son, and Julia was bored...'

'Hush...' Caroline soothed, hoping that Lavender would fall asleep soon and the feverish flow of words would cease. She doubted that the girl would even remember them in the morning.

'And then Andrew died and Julia was most put out,' Lavender said, with some satisfaction, 'but there was always Andrew's friend Jack Chessford—with Julia there is always the friend... I do hope—I do *so* hope that Lewis will see through her, but I fear not...I saw him with her in his arms last night...'

Caroline felt icy cold. She too had secretly hoped that Lewis would see through Julia's outward beauty to the person beneath, for he was hardly a fool and she would have expected him to be a good judge of men. But of women...? Physical beauty could blind a man to much. Caroline had seen that plenty of times before and her heart, which had been in her boots, sank still further.

'I would like it above all things if Lewis would marry you, Caroline,' Lavender confided, smiling a little. 'I shall have to contrive...' and at last, she fell asleep.

Caroline sat beside her for a little, until the fire died down and the cold in the room made her shiver. She got up and moved across to the grate, adding coal and logs to build the fire up again so that Lavender should not awaken with the cold.

'Let me help you with that.'

The door had opened softly and Lewis Brabant came back into the room. He helped Caroline to her feet and bent down to stir up the fire, before straightening up and casting a critical look over her.

'You look cold, Miss Whiston, and tired.' He kept his voice low. 'I see that Lavender is asleep now. I hope that she was not…too…distressed.'

Caroline thought that it was hardly the moment to mention that Lavender seemed most disturbed at the thought of her brother's marriage to Julia. 'Miss Brabant is very upset, of course,' she murmured. 'It is only natural. I believe she will sleep through the night, though. Cook put quite a measure of spirits in the milk…'

Lewis's tired face lightened a little. 'It sounds just the thing. I only hope it did not make her too loquacious first!'

Caroline avoided his eye. 'Not…not particularly, sir.'

Lewis raised an eyebrow and Caroline realised that something in her tone had given her away. She had always found it difficult to dissemble, particularly when she was feeling self-conscious, and the very knowledge that he was such a perceptive man made her feel even more ill at ease.

'I see.' Lewis sounded amused. 'Never fear, Miss Whiston! I shall not ask you to break my sister's confidence! Now, you must be tired. I'll bid you good-night.'

They went out together, Lewis raising a casual hand in farewell as he went downstairs. Caroline went to her room and prepared for bed, but found that she could not sleep. The sponge cake was sitting heavily on her stomach and her mind was full of the events of the day. She took out a book and read for a little, then sat by the window looking out at the dark and listening to the muted sounds of the household. Gradually the house became quiet. Caroline heard the clock in the hall strike one. She cast her book aside with a sigh and decided to go down to the kitchens for a third time, this time for a drink for herself.

Pulling a woollen wrap over her nightdress, Caroline slipped out on to the landing. There was no one about. She was not superstitious, but the shadows and the silence made her suddenly nervous and she averted her eyes from the closed door of the Admiral's room. She hurried down the stairs, her candle held high in one hand, the other grasping the wooden banister. A light still showed beneath the door of the study but there was no sound from within the room.

Caroline was about to tiptoe towards the door to the servants' quarters when a movement caught the corner of her eye. The candle flared as she spun round and she gave a muted squeak of alarm. She thought she saw the faintest of shadowy figures waft away down the corridor, then the light went out as her candle fell from her shaking hand.

Chapter Six

The study door opened with an abrupt crash.

'What the devil is going on there?' It was Lewis's voice, sharp out of the darkness. He came out into the hall, holding his own candle high. 'Miss Whiston? What the deuce—'

Caroline's teeth were chattering with nerves. 'I beg your pardon, sir. I saw… I thought I saw someone in the hall…a figure in grey…'

Lewis caught her arm and pulled her unceremoniously into the study. Caroline's relief at being in the light again was tempered a moment later by the sudden realisation that she was in her night attire and that she was now alone in the room with Lewis. She turned to face him and saw that he too was in a state of undress scarcely suitable for company. He had discarded his jacket and cravat, both of which were cast carelessly over the back of one of the chairs, and his shirt was open at the neck. The candlelight gilded his skin to deep bronze and shadowed his blue eyes. Caroline felt her throat dry with an entirely different type of nervousness. Her gaze moved to the half-empty brandy bottle that was standing on the desk, and at the same moment she heard the door close behind her with a wholly unnerving click.

'Have no fear, Miss Whiston,' Lewis said smoothly, reading Caroline's mind with an accuracy she was beginning to find very disturbing. 'Though appearances may be to the contrary, I am quite sober. Pray take a seat and tell me what has alarmed you.'

He put the candle down on the desk and turned to look at her. Caroline's hand strayed to her throat in a nervous gesture. She could think of nothing but that she was in her nightdress and her hair was loose about her shoulders, and she must look like the veriest cyprian.

'I think I had better not, sir.' She found that her voice was still a little unsteady. 'It was only my foolish imagination. I was feeling uneasy and thought I saw an apparition—'

'The grey lady.' Lewis strolled over to the side table and splashed some brandy into a glass. He held the bottle up. 'Are you sure you will not join me?'

'Quite sure, I thank you, sir.' Caroline knew she sounded prim and heard him laugh a little mockingly.

'Then take a seat at least, Miss Whiston, and bear me company.' Lewis came across and sat down, gesturing to Caroline to join him. He crossed his legs at the ankle and leant back. 'I need some company tonight. I do believe that you have seen our resident ghost.'

'The grey lady?' Caroline sat down a little

abruptly. 'Surely not, sir! Ghosts and spirits—what nonsense!'

Lewis shrugged lightly. 'I am surprised that you have not come across the tale in your reading, Miss Whiston! Apparently the lady in question was the wife of a royalist who lost his life in the civil war. When she heard of his death she was inconsolable and refused to eat. She wasted away until she died, and now she haunts the house and gardens, flitting about like a grey shadow whenever there is a death in the family.'

Despite herself, Caroline shivered. 'Stuff and nonsense!' she said stoutly, wrapping her arms closely about herself as she tried to get warm. 'It is just a fanciful story!'

Lewis laughed. He took a long draught of brandy. 'Practical Miss Whiston! Yet you were the one who saw her…'

Caroline shivered again.

'Come closer to the fire,' Lewis said softly. His eyes were intent on her face, making Caroline feel even more tinglingly ill at ease. 'We should not frighten ourselves with ghost stories on winter nights.'

'I would have thought that you would have no time for such foolishness, sir!' Caroline said astringently, assuming a brisk manner to cover her discomfiture. 'Surely you are more used to dealing with matters of action rather than imagination!'

Lewis stretched. Caroline saw the muscle ripple beneath the white linen of his shirt and tore her gaze away. Suddenly the room felt a lot warmer, rather hot and cold at the same time, which was confusing. Caroline wondered if she was about to contract a chill.

'Surely you have heard that seafarers are the most superstitious breed imaginable, Miss Whiston!' Lewis said sardonically. 'We can always be relied upon to tell the most fearsome tales! But let us change the subject. Tell me instead how you came to be wandering about the house so late.'

'I could not sleep,' Caroline said evasively. 'I thought to fetch myself a cup of milk. In fact,' she jumped up, 'that is what I will do now!'

Lewis looked her over with lazy amusement. His gaze took in her flushed cheeks and seemed to linger on the rich chestnut hair that curled about her face. 'What, dare you brave those dark corridors alone?'

'I am persuaded that I imagined the whole matter!' Caroline said briskly. 'There is no danger!'

'Probably less than staying here with me,' Lewis said. His gaze, dark blue as the summer sea, drifted over her again, making her feel acutely uncomfortable. It was not an unpleasant awareness, Caroline thought a little breathlessly, but rather one loaded with too many unnerving feelings. She did not want to think about it, for already she felt as thought she was straying perilously out of her depth.

Lewis reached for the brandy bottle again. 'Well, if I cannot persuade you to join me in a nightcap—'

'I think not,' Caroline said politely, 'but I thank you.' She retreated towards the door, her sense of relief increasing with every step she took. It was only when her hand was actually on the latch that a horrid thought struck her and made her pause. Supposing the Captain intended to sit here all night and drink himself into oblivion? The loss of his father could well take him that way, and though he had shown nothing but strength in supporting Lavender thus far, how would his sister feel if she awoke the next day and found Lewis insensible with drink?

'You hesitate, Miss Whiston.' Lewis's mocking tones broke into her thoughts. He got to his feet and moved towards her with the loose-limbed grace that was peculiarly his own. There was a teasing glint in his eye. Caroline backed away, her gaze riveted on his face.

'Oh…no, it was simply that I concerned that you might—' She stopped, torn between her anxiety and the realisation that she could be getting herself into trouble.

Lewis smiled a little. 'You are concerned that I am more than a little adrift and that without your restraining influence I will become positively foxed?' His smile deepened. 'Well, you may be correct on the first point, Miss Whiston, but you may also trust me… I shall not let Lavender down.'

'I did not think that you would,' Caroline said, as coolly as she was able. 'I admire you for the support you have given your sister, but often it is those who care most about others whom no one else thinks to comfort—' She broke off, the colour flooding her face as she saw the expression in his eyes, a mixture of tenderness and amusement.

'That is very true, Miss Whiston,' Lewis said slowly, 'for you could be speaking of yourself! For all your brusque façade, you care much about others do you not? But who cares for you? You must have been lonely…'

Caroline felt her grasp of the situation slipping away. He was very close to her now. She could almost imagine that she could smell the scent of his skin, feel the warmth emanating from his body. Such thoughts made her feel slightly faint and she struggled to regain her usual cool common sense.

'You mistake me, I meant nothing so profound,' she said hurriedly. 'I was only alarmed that you might over-indulge—'

Lewis's smile told her that he did not believe her. 'I am touched that you seek to comfort me, Miss Whiston.'

'Such was not my intention!' Caroline said, a little wildly. She turned back towards the door. 'You twist my words, sir! I must go! I am very tired!'

'Not so fast, Miss Whiston,' Lewis murmured. His arm slid around Caroline's waist, pulling her against him. There was no time for her to think; his mouth was on hers, for a moment soft and sweet, then hard and demanding. Caroline felt herself tremble, leaning the palms of her hands against his chest to steady herself. She could feel the beat of his heart, taste the hint of brandy on his lips. A hundred protests came into her head and fled beneath the touch of his hands. He was tangling his fingers in the heavy fall of chestnut hair about Caroline's shoulders, and now she could feel him stroking the nape of her neck so softly that she shivered with pleasure. The gentle touch was acutely at odds with the ruthless skill of his kiss. Caroline's tiredness mingled with a most delicious weakness, creating a sensual lassitude that robbed her of the will to move.

'Dear Caro…' Lewis said softly, when his lips left hers. His vivid blue gaze scanned her face and his eyes darkened with desire again. 'I have so wanted…'

His hand came up to touch her cheek lightly, sliding beneath her chin and turning her lips up to his again. This time the kiss was gentle, the searching urgency held in check. Lewis's grip tightened and Caroline slid her arms about his neck, pressing closer against him. She was dazed and dazzled, swept by such unfamiliar feelings…

A door closed stealthily nearby. It was a small noise, but enough to bring Caroline to her senses. How many people knew that she had come downstairs, that she was alone in the study with the master of the house? Suddenly what had seemed so sweet and precious became sordid. The master of the house and the governess companion… It conjured up all sorts of cartoon images in Caroline's mind, the whispered gossip of the servants, the smirks and knowing looks… She pulled herself out of Lewis's arms and drew her wrap more closely about her, clearing her throat painfully.

'I believe you took more than mere comfort there, sir…'

Lewis's eyes were very dark. He ran a hand through his dishevelled fair hair. 'Miss Whiston, I—'

'Pray do not apologise, sir!' Caroline said quickly. She did not think she could bear it if he made matters worse by telling her it was all a mistake, a drunken error of judgement.

'I was not planning to do so.' Lewis gave her a very straight look. 'I wanted—' He broke off and rubbed a hand across his brow. 'Confound it, this is not as I had intended—'

Caroline pressed her fingers against her lips. Suddenly, like a dose of cold water, she remembered Lavender telling her that she had seen Julia in Lewis's arms only the previous day. Abruptly, Caroline's mortification turned to icy anger within her. She had been in danger of losing her heart, whilst he…

'Embracing several different women in a short space of time must have its difficulties,' she observed coldly. 'May I suggest that you rein in your rakish tendencies, sir? You will find life so much less confusing that way!'

Lewis stood still, looking at her with raised eyebrows. 'Rakish tendencies? My dear Caroline—'

'I did not give you permission to use my name, sir, nor do I wish to be treated as some kind of rival to Julia for your affections!' Caroline said, unable to contain herself. 'It may amuse you, but I consider it an inappropriate jest!'

'A jest? A rival to Julia? Whatever can you mean?' Lewis looked genuinely puzzled and Caroline was incensed at his duplicity.

'Do you deny that *she* was the recipient of your attentions only yesterday? You are somewhat fickle, sir!'

Lewis' blue eyes narrowed on Caroline's face. 'What is this, servants' gossip? I do deny it!'

'The whole household knows of it!' Caroline said, exaggerating wildly, 'and it does you no credit to refute it, sir!'

There was some flash of expression in Lewis's eyes, so quick that Caroline could not read it, then he shrugged and his face went blank.

'Very well, Miss Whiston.' He spoke quietly. 'If that is how you wish it…' He handed her the candle from the desktop, then stepped forward and held the door open for her. There was no mistaking her dismissal. Caroline risked one further look at his face, but it was quite unreadable. He gave her a slight bow, as though encouraging her to be on her way, and closed the door behind her with a very decisive thud.

Caroline found herself out in the dark hall, all thought of a soothing drink fled. She wanted to do nothing more than run up the stairs and indulge in a hearty bout of tears to relieve her feelings. As a governess companion she was accustomed to ignoring slights, ill-natured comments and malicious tricks, but she had no experience of dealing with the kind of feelings that Lewis Brabant stirred up in her.

Caroline lay awake for the best part of the night. By dawn, her first fury with Lewis had abated into a

numb acceptance that she was partly to blame for
what had happened between them. She was the one
who had gone wandering about the house at night and
she had gone into the study even when she had seen
that he was alone. It was the action of a naïve débutante rather than a sensible woman of eight-and-
twenty. More to the point, she had scarcely fought
Lewis off when he had taken her in his arms. A part
of Caroline burned with shame when she remembered
the abandoned fashion with which she had returned
his kisses, but another part shivered at the memory of
his touch. She could hardly fool herself that she was
indifferent to him. She furiously told herself that he
was unprincipled and beneath contempt, but her heart
told another story.

The truth of the matter was terrifying to her and
she tried not to think on it too much. Caroline knew
that she had repressed her emotions for so long that
they were as dry as a tinderbox, and she was in serious danger of falling ever deeper in love. It was
inappropriate and pointless and yet another reason
why she had to leave Hewly as soon as possible.
Though she had lost her heart, Caroline saw no reason
to lose her head as well. She was not one to throw
her bonnet over a windmill, and to go to Lewis and
beg for his love was out of the question.

She finally fell asleep, to be woken late the next
morning by a housemaid with a can of hot water and
a tray of breakfast. Since Caroline had never had
breakfast in bed in the time she was at Hewly, she
was rather startled.

'Begging your pardon, miss,' the maid said in answer to her question, 'but the master insisted. He said that you had been up late caring for Miss Lavender and should have some time to rest.'

Caroline inwardly raised her eyebrows at this evidence of Lewis's thoughtfulness, lay back against her pillows and helped herself to a cup of chocolate. She was aware of a very definite and cowardly urge to avoid him that morning, but she knew it was impossible. With a sigh she got herself out of bed and had a thorough wash. She dressed in her undergarments, then lingered before her dressing-table, considering.

She was forced to concede that her figure was not bad when she did not choose to conceal it beneath drab worsted. She was slim but well-proportioned, although she knew she was considered rather tall for a woman. Society did not think of height as an attractive feature in a female, although for a governess it was a positive advantage as it gave an impression of authority. The rules of fashion did not really apply to governesses, Caroline thought suddenly. In fact, other women seemed offended if an upper servant was too attractive, and with the men it was positively dangerous.

She scrutinised her face in detail. Her lips were too full for beauty, though in repose they curved pleasingly into a hint of a smile. Her nose was snub, or retroussé, as her grandfather had affectionately called it. Her skin was good and her eyes a wide, clear hazel. Caroline let a lock of chestnut hair slide gently through her fingers. Once upon a time it had been dressed in ringlets and curls, falling about her face, or drawn up in circlets and ribbons. Such a very long time ago...

What could it be that drew Lewis Brabant's attention to her? Boredom, perhaps, or a sense of devilment. Caroline shook her head and pulled on a no-nonsense grey dress. She wound the curly chestnut hair into a particularly severe knot, and went downstairs.

The house was very quiet. There was no one in the drawing-room or the library, and Caroline was thinking reluctantly that perhaps she should go and find Julia when a noise on the gravel sweep outside attracted her attention. She walked over to the bay window and pulled aside the heavy curtain.

Lavender was standing some twenty feet away, deep in conversation with Barnabas Hammond. Barnabas had evidently come to deliver the mourning attire, for his hands were full of black silk scarves and crêpe bands, and a basket at his feet contained bonnets, caps, hose, handkerchiefs and other items all trimmed with black. Neither Lavender nor Barney were concentrating on the funeral attire, however, for they were quite engrossed in each other. Caroline drew back, concerned not to be seen prying, but as she turned away from the window there was a step behind her and she swung round to confront Lewis Brabant.

Caroline had had no time to prepare herself and felt at a definite disadvantage. Along with her own embarrassment, however, was a confusion over whether she should try to prevent Lewis from seeing the scene outside the window. If Lavender was gaining some solace from talking to Barney Hammond, Caroline could see no reason to interfere. Her brother might well feel differently, however.

As she hesitated, Lewis said, with rueful amusement, 'Do not worry, Miss Whiston! It would be a harsh brother indeed who wrests from his sister some comfort in the current situation! I am not inclined to intervene.'

'Oh! You knew!' Caroline let her breath out in a long sigh. She moved away, wanting to put some space between the two of them. Once again, she knew that her face had betrayed her thoughts. Still, if Lewis thought that her nervousness arose from concern over Lavender's situation rather than her own, she had at least managed to conceal something from him.

Whatever the ill-effects Lewis might be suffering from imbibing too much brandy the previous night, they were not visible to an onlooker. The stark black of the mourning clothes made him look uncompromisingly severe, and though his eyes were still tired, their gaze was quite steady.

'Before you run away, Miss Whiston, I should like to say something,' he said quietly. 'It will not take much time.'

Caroline's heart sank. Running away was precisely what she wanted to do. She rested her hands on the back of one of the chairs and gripped tightly.

'I imagine that you must believe you have several

good reasons for leaving Hewly after last night,'
Lewis said. He seemed to be choosing his words with
care but he held her gaze quite deliberately. 'I suppose that I should apologise for my conduct—'

Caroline turned her face away, afraid that her feelings for him would be too obvious. 'You had been
drinking—' she began, but stopped as Lewis put a
hand over one of hers, forcing her to look at him.

'Not that much. Caroline, I—'

'Lewis?'

Julia's voice came from behind them, sweet but
with a faintly puzzled note. Caroline had not heard
her come in. 'Excuse me if I intrude—'

Caroline heard Lewis swear softly under his breath.
He dropped her hand abruptly and turned, shielding
her from Julia's gaze.

'Good morning, Julia. I shall be with you directly.'

'Excuse me,' Caroline murmured. She knew that
her cheeks were scarlet with embarrassment and did
not dare to look at Julia's face as she brushed past
her on her way to the door. As she hurried away, she
heard Julia's voice, light and teasing, 'Lewis, my
dear, must you be so kind to poor Caro? She has led
a sheltered life, you know, and is in serious danger
of falling desperately in love with you, poor girl!'
And her peal of laughter followed Caroline up the
stairs, seeming to echo mockingly around the corridors and pursue her wherever she went.

Much to Caroline's surprise, Julia did not broach
with her the subject of the scene in the library.

Caroline could only assume that Julia was so sure of her power and so disparaging of any rival that she felt no need to mention it. As to what Lewis had been about to say, Caroline thought that it must have been an apology and told herself that she should be grateful that Julia had foreshortened so embarrassing a moment. She tried to avoid Lewis as much as possible, but it did not make for a comforting existence.

It was several days later that Caroline received a reply to her letter to Anne Covingham. Lady Covingham expressed her disappointment that matters had not fallen out well at Hewly, but was encouraging that she might be able to help Caroline find a place elsewhere. Friends of the Covingham family had just returned from India. They had a young family and two little girls just approaching the age when they required a governess. Anne would make enquiries on Caroline's behalf. Caroline folded the letter and put it in her chest of drawers, then, feeling a mixture of hope and obscure disappointment, went to find to Julia.

It was the morning of the Admiral's funeral, and Julia was seated at her dressing-table, brushing her hair slowly, whilst Letty shook out the black silk crêpe dress that she had been pressing. Julia's big blue eyes swept over Caroline's plain black bombazine, and she gave a slight nod.

'I should have guessed that you would have some old dress that would be appropriate, Caroline! You must have been in mourning for ever with all those dull families you have lived with! Still, I suppose that does not matter for a governess!' She stood up, stretched gracefully, and allowed Letty to slip the dress over her head. 'I was intending to purchase bombazet for you when the servants get new mourning clothes,' she said over her shoulder, 'but I see it is not necessary!'

Caroline helped Letty to fasten the hooks on the black silk dress, wondering if Julia expected to be thanked for her back-handed generosity.

'Will the crêpe be warm enough, Julia?' she enquired levelly. 'It is a chilly morning and the church will not be heated—'

Julia shrugged airily. 'Oh, it will do! To tell the truth I have a black grosgrain that would be warmer, but it is not near so pretty! And with my cloak and muff I shall do very well!'

She sat down to allow Letty to adjust the delicate black bonnet with its gauzy veil. 'What a gloomy way to start a new year! I declare, it is all silence and long faces! I quite yearn for some excitement! And Lewis has decreed a quiet funeral, so I shall have no one to gossip with!'

'I am sure that all the local families will pay their respects,' Caroline said tightly.

'Oh, surely,' Julia pirouetted about the room, and smiled with satisfaction as she heard the crêpe rustle about her, 'but you know that Lady Perceval scarcely deigns to acknowledge me! That must change when I am Mrs Lewis Brabant of Hewly Manor! I shall be generous, however, and not remind her of her former coldness!'

Lewis Brabant closed the study door behind him and leant against it for a moment in grateful silence. They had buried his father with the quiet dignity that the Admiral himself had requested in his last communication to his son. The Reverend William Perceval had led the simple and moving service, and many of the villagers had come to pay their last respects. Now the house was empty, the last of the mourners departed, and the Admiral laid in the cold earth beside his wife, his grave stark and newly turned amidst the snow.

The Admiral's final letter was before Lewis on the desk, forwarded by the family lawyer with a note to the effect that Mr Churchward hoped to present himself at Hewly within a few days to discuss the matter of the will. Admiral Brabant's instructions for his funeral rites had been quite specific. Since he could not be buried at sea, he would be interred with the minimum fuss and expense. Lewis smiled a little as he reread the close-written scrawl. His father's personality came over strongly; opinionated, terse, but for all that, a man to be respected.

He replaced the letter on the desk top and reached for the brandy bottle, frowning a little ruefully as he reflected that he had consumed more brandy in the last week than in a whole month in the Navy. Perhaps that was what had made his judgement so damnably at fault in the matter of Caroline Whiston. He had known what he wanted but had not thought how best to achieve it, and now he was presented with a whole new set of problems...

'Lewis?'

He turned to find that Julia was in the doorway. The light was behind her, and she appeared shadowy and insubstantial in her black crêpe dress. She glided forward into the room and closed the door quietly behind her.

'Pray do not let me disturb you, Lewis,' she said with a gentle smile. 'I know you will wish for some time alone to think of your father. I merely wanted to say goodnight.' She looked at him with sorrowful eyes. 'Poor Uncle Harley. It made me so sad to see him suffer so much. For all our differences, I loved him dearly.'

Lewis rubbed a weary hand across his eyes. He had no particular desire for a tête-à-tête with Julia, but he knew she was trying to tell him something and it seemed discourteous to dismiss her.

'My dear Julia, whatever can you mean? I had no notion that you and my father did not see eye to eye! What can he have done to upset you?'

He saw her hesitate before she made a gesture of denial, a fluttering motion of the hands that was as charming as it was distressful. Her voice was full of confusion.

'To own the truth, Lewis, I always intended to tell you, but not just yet—' She looked up and met his eyes, and her own were full of mortification. He took a swift step towards her, but she moved away, evading his gaze. 'Oh, let us not speak of it! Not now, of all times!'

Lewis was aware of feeling irritated. He schooled his features to patience and took both her hands in his. 'Julia! If there is something I should know—'

She tried unsuccessfully to free herself. 'Oh it is nothing! I feel so ashamed of speaking of it!' She gave a little shudder. 'It was all so long ago, and no doubt I mistook the situation—'

'Julia!' Lewis gave her a little shake. He was feeling both annoyed and concerned now. What could his father have done to engender such embarrassment? And why should Julia be so wary of telling him?

Julia gave a graceful little shrug. 'Oh, if I must tell you…' She cast her eyes down.

'You may remember, Lewis, that when you went to sea I was quite desperately in love with you and hoped that we might marry.' She raised her gaze to his suddenly. Her eyes were limpid and very blue, and Lewis felt a pang of some emotion he did not wish to analyse. 'Despite the fact that our betrothal was a secret I felt as bound by it as if—' She broke off, biting her lip. 'But that is immaterial. What you must have thought when you heard I was promised to Andrew, I cannot imagine.' Her tone was anguished. 'It was your father's doing, Lewis! He made me agree to marry your brother! He told me directly that it was a business matter, uniting two fortunes and that I was a foolish chit to imagine otherwise! And your brother was as determined as he! Together they wore me down, and I was so very young and alone…'

She freed herself and moved away from him. Lewis watched her as, head bent, she stared into the fire. His first response, a natural anger, was already fading into a cynical acceptance. His father had been an ambitious man whose plans for his children had involved both the augmentation of his wealth and social advancement. It was no surprise to hear that his strategy had involved keeping a grip of Julia's fortune.

Julia was watching him, and for a moment Lewis thought he glimpsed a flash of a strange expression in her eyes, too swift to read. She straightened up and gave him a smile that was both brave and shaken.

'Poor Lewis! I am so very sorry to tell you this when your father is scarce cold in his grave, but I thought it better to be honest…'

He had not noticed until now just how close she was to him. One—or both—of them must have moved instinctively towards the other. Julia's face was tilted up to him, the luscious red lips parted slightly. He could smell her perfume, faint but sweet. After a moment, she said regretfully, 'There is worse I fear, my dear. When your brother died before we could be wed, your father suggested that he take the place of the bridegroom—'

This time, the shock was so sudden that Lewis felt it hit him like a physical blow. He could not imagine what must be showing on his face. Julia was watching him with concern and she put a light hand on his arm.

'Lewis…'

Lewis took a deep breath. 'I cannot believe… You are saying that *my father* intended to marry you when his plans came to naught? But he… My mother had died only days before of the same fever that carried Andrew off—'

Julia evaded his eyes again. A faint shade of colour had come into her cheeks. Lewis knew that his pain and repulsion were clear in his voice, but he could not help himself. He broke away and strode across the room, as though to dissipate the horror with action.

'Good God, the squalor of it! How could he—'

Julia had followed him. He could feel her presence close behind him. In an agony of revulsion he swung round and caught her arms. The first allegation he could well believe, for the Admiral might well have forced her to marry Andrew in an attempt to keep the money in the family. But the second? For all his faults, the Admiral had been as sincerely attached to his well-born wife as she was to him and he had been too scrupulous a man to sink to marrying his own ward. Surely…

Lewis looked down into Julia's clear blue eyes. There was nothing there but anguish and he had an unnerving conviction that she must be telling the truth. Besides, why should she lie? There was nothing to gain.

'I am so sorry, Lewis.' Julia's words were a whisper. 'I would have spared you this, but I needed you to know the truth. It was the reason I married Jack Chessford, you see, and in such unseemly haste… I had to escape. But it was always you that I loved…'

Lewis stared down into the exquisite face so close

to his own. His mind was cloudy with tiredness, re-coiling from the horror of what he had heard. He felt Julia press closer to him, softly brushing the length of her body against his.

A stray breath of wind stirred the letter on the desk and stirred at the same time some doubt in Lewis's mind. It had something to do with letters, but the connection evaded him, slipping away. Nevertheless he froze. Julia, nestling close, opened her eyes.

'Lewis?' she whispered.

He put her away from him gently, aware of a sudden and extraordinary sense of distaste. Caroline Whiston's face was before his eyes; the uncompromising honesty of her gaze, the sweetness of her smile on the rare occasions she could be tempted from her severity, the softness of her mouth beneath his… He stood back punctiliously.

'Julia. Excuse me. I am very tired.'

He could see the chagrin in her eyes but before she could speak the front door bell jangled violently. They both stood quite still for a moment.

'The mourners have all gone home,' Julia began crossly. 'Who could possibly wish to call now?'

Lewis went over to the door and flung it open. 'Marston? What the devil's going on?'

The front door was wide and a quantity of luggage was being unloaded from the carriage outside and piled on the steps. Lewis strode forward.

'What the deuce—'

'You're not on the quarterdeck now, Lewis,' Richard Slater's voice said sardonically. 'A fine welcome this is for your old friend!'

Chapter Seven

Caroline splashed through the puddles on the road from Abbot Quincey to Steep Abbot. The first snow-fall of winter was thawing, but local soothsayers were promising another cold snap. In the meantime, Caroline found that her boots were leaking and her cloak was soaked through at the hem.

She had been into the main village to send some letters and pick up a few bits and pieces for Julia, and now she was hurrying back as the winter light faded and the darkness set in across the fields. It had been pleasant to be out of the house; Lewis and Richard Slater had been out on the estate all day, Lady Perceval had swept Lavender away to the Hall for a few hours, and Julia had been cross and scratchy as a consequence of being left behind again.

'Miss Whiston!'

Caroline had just passed the last cottage on the edge of Abbot Quincey when she was hailed by Mr Grizel, who was emerging through a doorway at the end of what had evidently been a pastoral visit. The curate trod eagerly down the path towards her, cassock flapping, his gaunt visage wreathed in smiles. For all her charity, Caroline could not help feeling that he looked like a crow. She organised her face into some semblance of a welcoming smile, and waited for him beside the picket fence.

When Mr Grizel arrived he was somewhat out of breath.

'Apologies for greeting you like that, ma'am,' he puffed, bowing awkwardly. 'I saw you pass by and wished to beg a word...' Here he was obliged to break off for a moment to regain his breath.

'I had a plan, ma'am, an excellent idea,' the curate burbled on. 'Knowing of your undoubted skill in encouraging youth in the ways of virtue and good education, I wondered if I might make so bold—' Mr Grizel temporarily lost himself in his circumlocution. Caroline raised her eyebrows and waited.

'The village school, Miss Whiston!' Mr Grizel waved his arms about enthusiastically. 'Might I prevail upon you to spare a little of your time for the children? The benefits of a sound education for untutored minds, the influence of culture and instruction—'

'I should be delighted, Mr Grizel,' Caroline said hastily, fearing that the curate was about to launch into a lecture. 'If you feel I could be of help—'

Mr Grizel beamed. 'Dear Miss Whiston! I knew I could rely upon you to spread the light! Where there is darkness—'

'Indeed,' Caroline said, seeing an opportunity to

escape. 'Speaking of which, sir, I must be on my way. The evening is drawing in.'

Mr Grizel seemed disinclined to bid her farewell. He came out on to the road and kept pace with her, asking after the household at Hewly and commiserating over the Admiral's sad demise. Caroline responded civilly and it was only where the track petered out into a narrow path that she turned to him and held out her hand in an unmistakable sign of dismissal.

'Our ways must part here, I believe, sir. Good day to you—'

To her amazement her hand was grasped in a fervent grip.

'Miss Whiston!' Mr Grizel's Adam's apple bobbed nervously. 'My *dear* Miss Whiston! I had intended to wait a while longer, but your wholehearted agreement to my plans has led me to believe… I *know* you are the helpmeet I require! Allow me to tell you how ardently I admire you!'

Caroline blinked. She tried to free herself, but Mr Grizel was more tenacious than he looked and hung on to her hand with grim determination. Worse, he suddenly went down on one knee on the path in front of her.

'Be mine, admired Caroline! May I be greatly daring and call you thus? Consent to be my wife and make me the happiest of men! Only say the word—'

'I fear that the word is no, sir,' Caroline began. This was worse than her worst imaginings, comic but sad at the same time. She tried to extricate herself once more. 'I am deeply honoured, but I fear I must decline—'

'But why?' Mr Grizel wailed in anguish. 'Surely it is more favourable than your current situation? I am not without means—'

'Please, sir,' Caroline said quickly, wishing to spare both of them embarrassment, 'say no more! We should not suit! And pray get up! You are kneeling in a puddle and someone is coming!'

'Time,' Mr Grizel pressed on hopefully, covering her hand with moist kisses. 'All ladies need time to consider an offer! I shall—'

'Pray, sir, desist!' Caroline said forcibly. She abandoned all hope of sparing his feelings. He really was an irritatingly persistent man and perhaps he deserved to be snubbed after all. She pulled on her hand; he pulled back. Caroline slipped on the damp grass by the path and managed to twist herself from his grip. And at the same time there was a clatter of hooves on the path, a muffled oath from the approaching rider, and the horse missed the prostrate curate by less than a foot.

Mr Grizel scrambled up, but the rider had already flung himself from the saddle and lifted the unlucky cleric clear of the ground. Mr Grizel was not a small man, but dangling in Lewis Brabant's fearsome grip made him appear rather puny. Lewis let him go as suddenly as he had pounced on him, and Mr Grizel staggered over to the wall and leaned rather heavily against it. Caroline found her voice.

'Captain Brabant! You cannot treat a man of the cloth in such a manner—'

It seemed, however, that Lewis was not moved by a spirit of brotherly love towards Mr Grizel. Ignoring Caroline's comment completely, he stepped threateningly towards the cowering curate.

'What can you mean by manhandling Miss Whiston in that outrageous manner, Grizel? Good God, I would have expected more self-control in a man of your stamp! And to conduct your amorous affairs in the middle of the road at dusk is downright foolhardy, let alone ridiculous!'

'Captain Brabant!' Caroline exclaimed again. 'How dare you, sir!' She was infuriated by his casual reference to amorous affairs, as though she were some tavern wench. She moved closer to the shrinking cleric. 'You are the one who should be apologising! Treating Mr Grizel as though he were some miscreant—'

'The gentleman would have suffered more if I had not been able to stop my horse in time!' Lewis said coolly, looking directly at Caroline for the first time. 'The next time you encourage a proposal, Miss Whiston, pray make sure that you choose a safer place or you will find that you are betrothed one moment and sped on your way to heaven the very next!' He stood back and gave Caroline a heavily ironic bow. 'But tell me, am I to wish you happy?'

Caroline glared at him. She had totally forgotten the cringing Mr Grizel, who was still trying to efface himself against the wall.

'No, you are not!' she said hotly. 'I could have managed the business perfectly well without your intervention, sir! I wish you would take yourself off!'

'I have no intention of leaving you at the mercies of this zealous suitor!' Lewis said derisively, his gaze pinning Mr Grizel to the spot. 'I will take you up with me as far as Hewly, Miss Whiston!'

'Ridiculous!' Caroline said roundly, her temper now as inflamed as his. 'There is no need! Mr Grizel will be on his way home and I can cut across the fields and be back before dark—'

'Whilst you are under my roof you are my responsibility, Miss Whiston,' Lewis said, with icy politeness. 'I beg you not to argue. Your servant, Grizel.'

Before Caroline had any idea what he was about, he had tossed her up on to the horse's back and swung himself up into the saddle behind her. It was all accomplished so smoothly that Caroline had barely drawn breath before Lewis had taken up the reins and turned Nelson's head for home.

'Put me down at once—' Caroline began childishly, but Lewis only laughed.

'What, do you prefer a cold walk home to a little time spent in my company?' he said softly in her ear. 'I thought, perhaps, that we might continue our discussion of your matrimonial plans!'

Caroline suddenly found that she could not have spoken even had she wanted to. His arms were around her, holding her with infinite care against his chest, and she could feel his breath stirring the tendrils of hair about her face. He arranged the folds of his cloak about her and the soft cloth, smelling of him, brushed her skin. The words dried in her throat, the anger draining from her like water evaporating.

'I am surprised that you rejected poor Grizel,' Lewis said, after a moment. 'He is one of the Oxfordshire Grizels, you know, and is accounted quite a catch. Besides, it would be a way out of your current circumscribed existence, so perhaps you will change your mind when you have had a little time to consider—'

'I think not, sir!' Caroline snapped, her annoyance rushing back at his presumption. 'Not that it is *any* of your business, but I would never make a marriage of convenience just to escape my situation!' She wriggled indignantly. 'A fine opinion you must have of me—'

'Steady,' Lewis instructed quietly, tightening his arms as she started to slide off the horse's back. 'Do not startle Nelson! He is of a most nervous disposition!'

'Nonsense!' Caroline said indignantly. 'I am sure the poor creature is as insensitive as you are, sir!'

She felt Lewis laugh. The sound was warm and disconcertingly intimate in the darkness. He spoke quietly. 'How is it possible that a lady so soft to the touch can have a tongue as sharp as a sacking needle?'

'Stop at once and put me down, sir!' Caroline said furiously, betrayed by the trembling of her own body. His words had stirred the memories in her, the feelings she had sworn to freeze out after their last encounter. It made her all the more angry. 'I do not have to heed your words—'

'Oh, but you do…' Lewis's voice was still little above a whisper. 'You are entirely trapped, are you not, Caroline? A novel experience for so self-sufficient a lady! Dear Caro…' He lingered over the words as he had done once before. 'Be calm. We are having such an enlightening conversation! You would not make a marriage of convenience and I am happy to hear you say so.'

'It is none of your concern, Captain,' Caroline said, trying to sound cold when her whole body was suffused with heat. 'You are unmannerly—'

'Yes, I know.' Lewis's sleeve brushed her cheek and Caroline bit her lip. Here, in the near-dark, pressed so close to him, she felt acutely vulnerable. 'We have spoken on this before,' Lewis continued. 'I have been away at sea too long and have no idea how to go on—'

'Nonsense!' Caroline snapped again. 'You know perfectly well how to behave, sir, you simply *choose* to be ill-mannered! It is shameful!'

'My dear Miss Whiston!' Lewis bent his head and his lips touched the corner of her mouth. They were cold against her cheek. 'I now feel precisely like one of your badly behaved charges! Or perhaps,' his voice changed, 'not *precisely* like one of them…'

Caroline was immensely grateful to see the lighted windows of the Manor approaching. She turned her head away and tried to still the traitorous weakness that swept through her. When they turned into the stableyard she was forced to wait until Lewis had dismounted and lifted her down in his arms, for she knew her legs were too shaky to support her. She tore herself from his grip and walked with head held high towards the door of the house. Lewis caught up with her as they crossed the gravel sweep. She thought that he said something—her name, perhaps—in an undertone shaken with laughter, but then the door was thrown open and Julia stood on the threshold. It was evident that she was in a towering rage.

'Caroline! Where have you been? I have been waiting these two hours past in need of your assistance with a letter—' Her gaze slid from Caroline's flushed face to Lewis's blank one and lingered there thoughtfully. There was a long pause, broken fortunately by Richard Slater's emergence from the library. He seemed blissfully unaware of any tension in the atmosphere.

'Lewis! Did you have a good ride back?'

'Eventful,' Lewis said expressionlessly. 'Would you care for a drink before dinner, Richard? I feel in need of one!' He bowed to Caroline and Julia. 'Ladies, pray excuse us—'

'Well, really!' Julia said, as the study door closed behind them. She seemed uncertain whether to vent her spleen on Caroline or Lewis. 'It's all of a piece as soon as there is another gentleman in the house!' She swung round sharply on Caroline. 'And what were you looking so guilty about, pray? You looked as thought you had been caught kissing in the shrubbery!'

Caroline was feeling decidedly out of sorts. 'I fear Captain Brabant had been ringing a peal over me for encouraging Mr Grizel's attentions,' she said, resorting shamelessly to half-truth and evasion. 'We had a most uncomfortable journey back.'

Julia clapped her hands, her good humour restored. 'Mr Grizel has made you an offer! I knew it! And have you accepted him, Caroline?'

'Certainly not!' Caroline said with dignity.

'I suppose that was why Lewis was so annoyed,' Julia said, with satisfaction. 'Really, Caro, you have no idea how to go on! Only fancy rejecting such a suitor! Why, Mr Grizel has a private income of ten thousand a year!'

'Sorry about last night, old chap,' Captain Slater said ruefully as he and Lewis took port after dinner that evening. 'As I said this morning, I had no intention of intruding on the day of the funeral! Fact is, I'd been up in Bath for a few days and your letter must have passed me on the road. If I'd known about your father's death I would never have come—'

Lewis made a swift gesture and cut him off. 'No apology required, Richard, I assure you. Truth is, I was glad to see you. Things have been damnably difficult here these last few weeks and some different company is most welcome.'

Richard flashed Lewis a grin. 'Well, if you're sure... To tell the truth, I've been waiting all day to hear about your petticoat government! I was uncertain whether I would find you here or decamped to London with the fair Mrs Chessford!'

Lewis gave Richard a look, his eyes narrowing. 'Not sure if I should call you to account for that remark, Richard!'

'Oh, I can do better than that!' Captain Slater said with a cheerful shrug. 'I have a special commission from Fanny to discover whether you are betrothed to Mrs Chessford! The tabbies of Lyme would be taking bets on it if they were not all too genteel to gamble!'

Lewis looked startled. 'How is it that my business is of such interest?'

Richard made a deprecating gesture. 'Fortune, old fellow! Estate! Single gentleman in need of a wife and all that!'

'How is it that you have escaped their attentions then?'

Captain Slater looked as soulful as one of his cheerful countenance could manage. 'Alas, I have a broken heart and am inconsolable!'

'The devil you are!' Lewis looked amused. 'It's the first I heard of it! Besides, surely there is some young lady who plans to cure you? To make you happy again!'

Richard grimaced. 'What a dismal idea! Remind me to develop a new strategy before anyone thinks of it! Anyway,' he cast his friend a sideways look, 'I may not remain heartbroken for ever.'

Lewis got up to stoke the fire. 'You would not be so unoriginal as to develop a *tendre* for Mrs Chessford yourself?'

'Not if you don't wish it, old chap! No, I had more in mind to fix my sights on the fascinating Miss Whiston!'

Lewis stopped in the act of passing the decanter. 'I beg your pardon?'

'Miss Whiston!' Richard Slater's grey eyes were bright with amusement as they dwelt on his friend. 'You referred to her as some Friday-faced female, if I recall correctly—'

'I think not!'

'Well, you did. But now that I have got to know her—'

'That was quick work—'

'Well, I was always renowned for it, if you recall! As I was saying, now that I have met her, I realise that you were fair and far out in your description! I thought last night that she looked like the goddess Juno, and she reads philosophy—'

Lewis swore. He returned the decanter to the desk with a decided thump. 'The goddess Juno? When did you see this apparition, Richard?'

'Last night, old chap, like I said! She was coming out of the library! I introduced myself at once!' Richard smiled reminiscently. 'She had a book of Sophocles under her arm and her hair was loose with the firelight shining through—'

He broke off at the martial light in his friend's eye. 'Your pardon, Lewis! Sits the wind in that quarter then?'

There was a silence but for the crackling of the

fire. Lewis looked up and met his friend's quizzical gaze.

'I believe you said all that on purpose,' he said mildly.

Richard grinned. 'Devil a bit! I should be happy to be at Miss Whiston's feet!'

'Well, don't be!' Lewis's frown returned. 'I have plans—'

Richard raised his hand in a gesture of surrender.

'Point taken! No need to call me out! Now, do you remember Charles Drew? Served with you on the *Neptune* under Freemantle? He was in port last week and called to see me…'

Lewis sat back and allowed himself to be drawn into reminiscence, but half his mind was elsewhere. Richard's words had prompted him to think again about the events of the previous night, but it was Julia rather than Caroline Whiston who occupied his thoughts. Something in Julia's statements about his father had not rung true, but at the time he had not been able to work out exactly what it was. Now he remembered. Julia had claimed that the Admiral had intended to force her into marriage and that she had eloped with Jack Chessford through necessity. Yet in the letter that Caroline had accidentally left in the poetry book, Julia had made some reference to her marriage, and it had been couched in entirely different terms…

If only he had read more of it! If only he could see the others… Lewis imagined Caroline's reaction if he asked her to let him borrow them, and smothered a smile. Then she would give him the rightabout and no mistake! Yet he had to know, for if Julia were telling the truth it would be one of the most painful discoveries he could make, but if she was lying…

He thought of Caroline then, of the sweetness hidden beneath the severity. What had Richard said? 'Her hair was loose with the firelight shining through…' Lewis shifted in his seat. Every so often there would be a tantalising glimpse of that creature of the woods that he had met on his first day home. Deny it as she might, Caroline Whiston was an intriguing conundrum.

Caroline was having a peaceful afternoon. Earlier that day, Julia had revealed a sudden need to travel to Northampton for some goods that Abbot Quincey could apparently not supply. Whether this sudden discovery had anything to do with Captain Slater's avowed intent to visit the town Caroline could not be sure, but certainly the Captain had declared himself delighted to escort her. Caroline wondered whether this was some ploy of Julia's to make Lewis jealous. Certainly she could not believe that Julia had decided to give up her pursuit of Lewis in favour of Richard Slater, who had a comparatively small competence and was decidedly less good-looking.

Caroline liked Captain Slater. He had a practical, good-humoured nature and treated her with exactly the same deference and charm as he did Lavender and Julia. Sometimes there was a decided look of admiration in his eyes when he spoke to her, but Caroline found that she was quite comfortable with this and that it did not disturb her in the same way that Lewis's perceptive regard was wont to do. Nevertheless, Caroline found herself hoping that Richard Slater would not fall prey to Julia's blandishments. The idea was a comical one in some ways—how many more of His Majesty's Navy needed protection against Julia's wiles?

Julia had only been gone a half-hour when Lady Perceval and her daughters and the Countess of Yardley came to call on Lavender. Caroline knew that it could only be coincidence that had brought them to Hewly as soon as Julia was absent, but she reflected that her erstwhile friend would fly up into the bows when she heard the news.

The January weather was unseasonably warm, al-most springlike, and Caroline had decided to take a stroll along the Little Steep river. She climbed a stile in the hedge and jumped down the other side, enjoy-ing the pale sunshine. Her mourning clothes were not very practical for walking and eventually she took off her bonnet and swung it by the strings, feeling rather like a young girl playing truant.

The path meandered along by the side of the river, which was narrow and deep at this point, running fast and brown with the recent thaw. Caroline rounded a bend, sheltered by coppiced willow, and stopped in surprise, for Lewis Brabant was sitting on the river-bank, his back against one of the trees. He had not seen her, for he was engrossed in his fishing, setting his line, his eyes narrowed with concentration.

Caroline watched him for a moment, undetected. As on that first evening at Hewly, she was struck by how much more relaxed he seemed in the freedom of the outdoors. When Lewis was inside the house it was almost as though there was some part of him that felt confined, held under forcible constraint. That was not to suggest that he did not look comfortable in the elegant drawing-rooms of society, for he had an easy assurance that would no doubt carry him through every situation. Despite that, however, Caroline thought he seemed happiest when he was not restrained by four walls.

She watched as he cast the line with one strong flick of the wrist then sat back against the tree. The fresh breeze ruffled his fair hair. Caroline felt as though a hand had squeezed her heart, then let her go, leaving her a little breathless. She made a slight, involuntary movement and Lewis looked up and saw her.

'Miss Whiston! Good afternoon, ma'am! Would you care to join me for a little?'

'Oh, pray do not get up, sir!' Caroline hurried forward to forestall him as he made to get to his feet. 'You will upset your line and you have just got it settled!'

Lewis subsided back against the tree trunk. 'I do believe that you have been watching me, ma'am,' he said slowly, his eyes travelling over her face with the searching intensity that made Caroline so aware of him. 'How long were you standing there?'

'A few moments only,' Caroline said hastily. 'I had

thought you at the Manor, entertaining your guests, sir!'

'I have left Lavender to do the honours,' Lewis said lazily, his eyes on the water. 'To tell the truth, Miss Whiston, drawing-room chatter holds little interest for me! A little conversation, to recognise the condescension of our noble visitors, and I was making my excuses! There is a short cut from Hewly gardens across the water meadows. It took me but a minute to reach this spot with my rod and line.'

'And now I have disturbed you,' Caroline said, making to walk on. 'I believe that fish dislike riverbank chatter as much as you dislike that of the drawing-room, sir!'

'Stay a moment,' Lewis said, gesturing to the rug spread out on the ground beside him. 'You need not speak to me! But it is pleasant to sit and watch the river run.'

After a moment's hesitation, Caroline sat down in the lee of a pollarded willow. The day was very quiet. Away in the distance she could see the roof of the Abbey, and she wondered idly what the Marquis of Sywell would do now that he was alone in all that splendour. The tale of the runaway wife had been the main gossip in the village for months now, with various wild stories circulating that the Marchioness had been gone for ages without anyone realising and, even more outrageous, that the Marquis had murdered her. Caroline sighed. Her own difficulties seemed to fade into insignificance when compared to the problems that would be faced by the Marquis's poor little wife.

Being alone in the world was a difficult business, as Caroline knew to her cost.

On the far side of the river a heron stood quite still in the shallows and a flock of woolly sheep grazed undisturbed. Lewis stretched, resting his fishing rod on a nearby stone.

'Sometimes it is pleasant to be still and think, is it not, Miss Whiston?'

'It is a luxury seldom allowed us,' Caroline agreed, with a little smile.

'Not everyone has the gift of silence,' Lewis said gravely, and for a moment Caroline wondered if he could be thinking of Julia. She turned her face away, feeling the faint sun warm her skin beneath the brim of her bonnet.

Lewis picked up a stone and idly skimmed it across the surface of the water.

'Miss Whiston, will you tell me something?' He hesitated. 'I wonder... Did Julia ever speak to you of her marriage?'

The question was sufficiently unexpected to make Caroline turn and look at him. He too was gazing out over the fields, his chin resting on his hand, some unreadable expression in his eyes. Caroline felt some of her contentment in the afternoon drain away.

'She wrote to me a little,' she said carefully. 'Why do you ask, sir?'

Lewis picked up the line again. 'I wondered if she had been happy,' he said.

Caroline bit her lip. Almost all her enjoyment of his company had now gone, since it seemed that

Lewis's only aim was to speak to her of Julia. She could have kicked herself for her folly in thinking that it could ever be otherwise.

'You would have to ask Mrs Chessford that your-self, sir,' she said, trying not to sound tart. 'I really have no idea. I believe that she enjoyed living in London and that Jack Chessford was an entertaining enough husband, but—'

'An entertaining husband…' Lewis mused. 'What do you consider would make a man such, Miss Whiston?'

Caroline set her lips in a thin line. Here was another of Lewis's strange, quixotic questions. She regretted ever making the remark.

'I have never needed to consider the matter, sir!' she said, not caring this time that she sounded sharp.

Lewis smiled at her suddenly and Caroline's heart gave a little erratic thump.

'Truly?' he asked. 'Well…' He shifted slightly. 'Tell me, Miss Whiston, have you kept all the letters that Julia sent you during your acquaintance?'

Caroline stared at him in amazement. She could not follow his train of thought at all.

'I believe so, sir. Again, I wonder at your enquiry!'

Lewis shifted again, as though he felt uncomfort-able. 'Forgive me, Miss Whiston. This questioning must seem odd to you, I know, but there is a reason… I wondered if Julia had ever given the impression that she did not feel happy…safe…at Hewly?'

Caroline stared. Evidently there was more to Lewis's enquiries than a simple wish to learn all he

could about his beloved's past, but she was at a loss
to understand the reason for his questions.

'I never gained that impression from her writing,'
she said, at length, 'but again I must urge you to apply
to Mrs Chessford directly, sir.'

Lewis's gaze came back from some distant point
and focused on her flushed face. He smiled at her
again.

'You are quite right, of course, Miss Whiston! I
should not have asked you. Forgive my importunity.'

Caroline made a slight gesture. She was quite at a
loss. 'It was nothing, sir.'

Lewis got to his feet and started to reel in his line.
'The fish are not biting today. I fear the river runs too
fast for them.' He looked down at her. 'Will you walk
back with me, Miss Whiston, or do you prefer that I
leave you to your solitude?'

Caroline stood up and dusted down her skirt. 'I will
walk back. Twilight is closing in already.'

'I think we are in for a colder spell,' Lewis observed, his gaze going from the sliver of rising moon
to the white mist that was starting to curl across the
water meadows. 'I should not be surprised if it snows
in a day or so!' He picked up his rod and line and
fell into step beside her.

The path followed the river's course for a little
way, then cut across the meadow and along the woodland edge until it reached the tumbledown wall that
marked the border of the Hewly estate. Now that the
sun had gone the air had a chill edge, and Caroline

shivered a little as they made towards the lighted windows of the house.

'It will just be the two of us for dinner tonight, Miss Whiston,' Lewis said suddenly, as they passed beneath the old apple trees. 'I believe that Julia planned to stay overnight with the Mountfords in Northampton, for there is a concert and assembly she wishes to attend. Richard,' his gaze was sardonic, 'apparently remains there also, to escort her back on the morrow.'

Caroline cast a glance at his face. It was impossible to tell whether he was disturbed to think of Julia already entangling his friend in her schemes. The twilight was deepening now, the sky pure dark blue overhead, and it cast Lewis's face in shadow.

'And Miss Brabant?' she questioned hesitantly. 'Does she not dine with us?'

Lewis flashed her a grin. 'Lady Perceval was intent on carrying Lavender off to the Hall for a few days! Oh, I know it is soon after my father's death, but I thought it the very thing for Lavender to have a change of scene... When I was leaving earlier—' he indicated the fishing tackle '—she was about to write you a note. I know she hopes you will visit her at Perceval Hall, Miss Whiston, for she would not wish to lose your company...'

Caroline was silent, prey to mixed emotions. Julia and Richard Slater absent, Lavender at Perceval Hall... She remembered the ride back from Abbot Quincey and shivered a little. It did not seem wise to entrust herself to Lewis's company.

'So we shall be all alone, Miss Whiston,' Lewis said gently, holding the garden gate open for her with scrupulous politeness. 'I cannot tell you how much I look forward to it!'

Chapter Eight

'Beg pardon, ma'am,' the little housemaid said nervously, 'but the Master says that he is waiting for you to take dinner!'

Caroline closed her book with a decided snap. Since her encounter with Lewis earlier she had been beset by a number of feelings, none of them comfortable. She had puzzled over his questions about Julia's marriage and her letters, had fretted over the thought of dining alone with him, and had eventually sent him a message to say that she would not be joining him and would take her meal alone in her room. It now seemed, however, that Lewis was not prepared to accept that decision.

'Pray tell Captain Brabant that I shall not be joining him,' she said sharply. 'The Captain already knows that I have excused myself!'

The maidservant screwed her eyes up in an agony of embarrassment and anxiety. 'Beg pardon, ma'am,' she said again, 'but the Captain said to tell you—'

she gulped '—that if you will not go to him he will come up here and dine with you in your bedroom!'

Caroline slapped the book down on her bed and got to her feet. 'Very well, Rosie, I shall come down! Do not look so worried, child—it is none of your fault!'

'No, ma'am!' The servant girl dropped a grateful curtsey and sped out of the room. 'Thank you, ma'am!'

Caroline hastily drew her black silk shawl about her shoulders and swept downstairs before her anger and indignation could desert her. Her outrage carried her as far as the hall, wavered slightly as a blank-faced footman held the dining-room door for her, and almost failed her altogether when she saw Lewis Brabant standing by the window and looking out over the dark garden. He turned as she came in and sketched a bow.

'Good evening, Miss Whiston! Thank you for joining me!'

'Is it your practice to send your servants with impertinent messages, sir?' Caroline asked frigidly. 'I had already sent to tell you that I did not wish to partake of dinner—'

'No,' Lewis corrected her affably, 'you had sent to tell me that you did not wish to take dinner with me! That is different!'

He came around the table to hold a chair for her. Caroline sat down, glaring at him. 'Very well! If we are not to mince our words, sir, it is true that I preferred to dine alone!'

'Thank you for that clarification! Perhaps you would explain why?'

Caroline struggled a little. 'Because it is inappropriate, sir!'

'Inappropriate,' Lewis murmured. 'Pray, Miss Whiston, is that one of your favourite words?'

Caroline ignored him. 'It is inappropriate for us to dine together when your sister and Mrs Chessford are absent—'

She was forced to stop as the door opened to admit a footman with the soup. When they had been served and the footman moved to take his place by the sideboard, Lewis signalled to him to withdraw altogether. Caroline caught her breath. For all that Lewis had listened to her views, he had evidently decided to disregard her feelings! This latest piece of irregular behaviour would have tongues wagging in the servants' hall!

Caroline applied herself to the food in silence. Since her remonstrations had cut no ice, it seemed that this was the only way to show her disapproval. Lewis, however, did not seem particularly abashed, for his smile had a teasing edge to it.

'I cannot really believe that we are outraging the tenets of polite society,' he observed gently. 'No doubt we shall have some pleasant conversation by and by, once you have overcome your annoyance that I forced your hand!'

Caroline glared at him again. Under such provocation, she was fast forgetting that one of her guiding principles was a cool and rational approach to all situations.

'You do not understand, sir,' she said coldly. 'You seem to enjoy deliberately flouting propriety! A governess companion should not—' She broke off again as the footman returned to remove the plates, and there was a heavy silence.

They were served with roast beef, and once again Lewis suggested that the man withdraw, adding a few words that were too low for Caroline to hear. When the door had closed behind him, Lewis looked at her and raised his eyebrows enquiringly.

'A companion should not—what—Miss Whiston?'

Caroline shot him a disapproving look. 'This is a waste of time, sir! You are clearly deaf to all pleas of respectability! I shall save my breath!'

'Ah, that argues a very practical mind! Why waste your time and energy on a lost cause?'

'That describes you very well, Captain!' Caroline agreed crossly. 'Determined, wilful—'

'Once again, I feel like one of your naughty charges, ma'am,' Lewis murmured. 'Do you also let them do as they please?'

'Certainly not!' Caroline frowned. 'I hope that they would be more conformable than you, Captain!'

Lewis laughed. He got up to pour her another glass of wine. 'I have certainly had longer to practise disobedience! But let us avoid such inflammatory topics! Tell me a little of the subjects you teach, ma'am.'

Caroline looked at him suspiciously. Surely no one was ever interested in the details of a governess's life?

'Oh, I teach all sorts of things!' she said. 'Languages and geography and music and drawing. If my charges cannot make landscapes in cut paper and embroider their own counterpanes and cushions, I feel I have failed at my task!'

'Landscapes in cut paper... You must be very accomplished yourself to be able to teach such things, Miss Whiston,' Lewis commented. 'But with Mrs Guarding's excellent schooling behind you...'

'Yes, indeed, I was most fortunate not to be turned out into the world without an education!' Caroline agreed with a slight smile.

'Yet there must be plenty of ill-educated governesses in the world, passing on their own ignorance!' Lewis observed, refilling her wine glass.

'Well, that is a little harsh,' Caroline found that she was laughing, 'but certainly there are those who struggle. And their charges are not always biddable girls!'

The conversation moved imperceptibly on to geography, then to history and politics, with Caroline lowering her guard as she realised that Lewis had a genuine interest in discussing such matters with her, as well as a well-informed mind. She found herself expressing her own views with an openness that was far from her usual demeanour.

When the footman finally returned to serve the dessert, Caroline realised that they had indeed been talking for a long time. She bit her lip. To relax into the intimacy of the situation, to find Lewis's company attractive and stimulating, would be a vast mistake. She refused the pudding course a little abruptly and hoped that Lewis would take the hint and go off to drink his port, allowing her to escape.

Lewis was frowning a little, as though he were aware of her withdrawal. 'I shall not desert you for the pleasure of the port,' he said, almost as though he had read her mind, 'for then I know you would run away! Pray come into the drawing-room for a little, Miss Whiston!'

Caroline hesitated. Lewis was coming round the table towards her and she suddenly felt a lot less sure of herself. With acres of polished wood between them she had not been so disturbed by his proximity, but now... He took her elbow in a firm grasp and Caroline felt a flicker of awareness ripple through her.

'I do not believe that would be quite—'

'Appropriate?' Lewis slanted a look at her.

'Suitable,' Caroline amended. She made a gesture of appeal. 'I am your cousin's companion, sir! Neither she nor your sister are at home, so...'

'So you said before! Am I to fear for my reputation? Is that it?'

Caroline looked reproachful. 'You may mock, sir!'

'Upon my honour, I intended to do no such thing! Is it not possible to be compromised by a governess companion? I could certainly try...'

'I scarce think so, sir,' Caroline said crossly. 'Though the reverse is undoubtedly true! Which is why I must have a care for my own reputation! Indeed, I am thinking of leaving Hewly shortly. Now that Miss Brabant is so well cared for, I feel free to take up another post.'

Lewis turned towards her, an arrested look in his eyes. His levity seemed forgotten.

'Must you go quite yet, Miss Whiston?'

'Well…' Caroline could feel a blush rising, 'I have the chance of a new position and I did plan…' She broke off, unwilling to refer back to the unhappy business of Julia's spiteful meddling.

'I suppose there is nothing to keep you here.' Lewis's voice was suddenly expressionless.

'Mrs Chessford does not really need a companion,' Caroline said, a little desperately, 'and you know that she and I do not really suit! I am sure that she has been very upset by the Admiral's death, but I cannot really offer her the solace she needs! She requires amusement and distraction, not someone to write her letters for her! And a change of scene would be useful— It must have been horrible for Julia that the Admiral was taken ill so soon after she arrived—'

Caroline stopped rambling, aware that Lewis's eyes had narrowed suddenly on her face. He had listened in silence as she had rattled on and somehow his intent gaze had made her chatter all the more, but now she fell silent as Lewis frowned.

'After she arrived, Miss Whiston? But surely Julia came to Hewly in response to my father's illness rather than before it!'

'Oh, no.' It was Caroline's turn to frown now. 'Nanny Prior told me that when Julia arrived, the Admiral was quite well! It was a few hours later that—' She broke off as she saw the flash of some extraordinary expression in Lewis's eyes. 'Why, what have I said, sir?'

Lewis was shaking his head slowly. 'Nothing, Miss Whiston. I am persuaded…' He touched her hand briefly, sending another shiver along Caroline's nerve endings. 'I wonder what else you know, however…'

For a moment his gaze searched Caroline's puzzled face. She forced herself to keep still beneath his scrutiny.

'About what, sir?' she asked coolly.

Lewis laughed. 'Pity me that I cannot ask you what is in my heart!' he said enigmatically. 'One thing I can ask you, however, Miss Whiston.'

Caroline raised her eyebrows enquiringly. 'Yes, sir?'

There was suddenly a spark of devilment deep in Lewis's blue eyes. Caroline's heart missed a beat.

'There is one thing that I envy my sister for, Miss Whiston,' he said slowly, 'and that is her friendliness with you where I must be formal—as you perceive, ma'am. May I not have a like privilege and address you by your name?'

'Oh!' Caroline pressed her hand to her throat. She remembered the caressing way in which Lewis had said her name on previous occasions, remembered suddenly the heat of his body against hers, the gentleness of his hands, the touch of his mouth… He had taken what he had wanted before. Now he was asking, but even so…

She moved away from him. 'No, Captain Brabant.

As I shall be leaving Hewly soon there is no necessity, and even were I to stay, that would be—'

'Inappropriate?' Lewis had followed her to the door. He did not touch her but to Caroline's over-stretched nerves the caressing effect of his voice was almost the same. 'Unsuitable?'

He put a hand on her arm as she made to escape.

'One day, Caroline,' he said, very softly, 'you will admit that under your very proper exterior is a most *inappropriate* governess. But until then—' he gave her a mocking bow '—I shall continue to address you as Miss Whiston. Goodnight, ma'am!'

He turned away and Caroline, regaining the use of her limbs, hurried out of the drawing-room and away to safety, without even waiting for a candle to light her way.

Caroline sat darning her second-best pair of black gloves and wondering what was to be done. She had spent another night tossing and turning, and for one who prided herself on sound sleep this was a dire sign indeed. The cause of her disturbance was, of course, Lewis Brabant, who had behaved in such an alto-gether quixotic and disconcerting manner the previous evening. It seemed unfair to Caroline that Lewis had immediately perceived the contradictions in her char-acter that she had successfully kept concealed for the whole of her adult life. He had swiftly seen that there were two Caroline Whistons; the staid governess companion who wore the grey worsted and acted so properly, and the free spirit who read poetry and dreamed of romance. Except that the free spirit was not truly free, for it had always been subject to the practical aspects of earning an unromantic crust. The sober lady's companion had always had the upper hand.

Caroline's thread snapped and she bit back an unladylike epithet. She knew it was her own fault, as she had been taking out her ill temper on the inoffensive darning. Casting it aside, she went over to the window. Her room was at the back of the house and had a view across the walled gardens to the rolling Northamptonshire countryside beyond. She could see two of the maids shaking out a blanket on the terrace below, and away down the gardens, Belton and Lewis Brabant were deep in conversation as they inspected the walls in the old rose arbour. Caroline sighed. It was pointless to wonder what quality had drawn her to Lewis in such a wholly inappropriate manner. Perhaps it was the contradictions in his own nature that had sparked such recognition in her. The authoritative man of action who was also dangerously perceptive… She shivered and drew back from the window, almost as though she thought her regard would draw his gaze.

Mrs Guarding had always said that action was the best cure for the blue devils, so Caroline took up her cloak and set out. She took care to avoid the gardens, walking down the path to the orchard and out on to the lane. It was a bright, frosty winter's day and her heart lifted a little with every step. She decided to make some calls.

Her first stop was the Guarding Academy itself. When Caroline had first returned to Steep Abbot, she had visited the school and had been made most welcome by Mrs Guarding. Her former teacher had delicately made no open reference to Caroline's change in circumstances but had chatted about the changes at the school and the activities of some of the other girls Caroline had known. She had returned to Hewly Manor with an open invitation to visit whenever she wished, but she had not taken this up, perhaps because the school held so many memories for her. When she had first thought of leaving the Manor she had considered Mrs Guarding as a possible employer, but now she knew that that would never serve. The school was far too close to Hewly and therefore to Lewis, and the thought of Julia holding court nearby as Mrs Lewis Brabant was more than Caroline's nature could take.

She rang the bell and discovered that Mrs Guarding was away, but received a very warm welcome from Miss Henrietta Mason, the history teacher. Caroline stayed for a cup of tea and enjoyed a long chat on the trials of trying to imbue young ladies with an interest in history and geography, which seemed to be the same whether taught in a private house or a forward-looking school. She finally left with a promise to visit Miss Mason again soon, and took the track towards Abbot Quincey.

Caroline turned aside from the road at Perceval Hall, as she had letters and messages for Lavender. She had not been intending to stay, but found herself invited to join the ladies in the saloon, and soon they were all chatting like old friends. After a while, Lavender suggested that Caroline accompany her to the church to lay a wreath on the Admiral's grave.

'I hope you do not feel my desertion too keenly, Caroline!' Lavender said as they walked along. 'Lady Perceval suggested that I should invite you to join me here, and if it were not for Julia—' She broke off. 'I am sorry. My tongue runs away with me when I speak of her! Tell me, has she prevailed upon Captain Slater to elope yet?'

Caroline gave her a reproving look that was marred by the twinkle in her eye. 'Lavender! You know you may well be speaking of your future sister-in-law!'

'I know it!' Lavender said gloomily. 'The whole neighbourhood knows it! I have been quizzed on little else!'

They let themselves in through the lychgate and walked slowly up the path to the quiet corner plot. There was a simple headstone and the grave still looked freshly turned. Caroline cast an anxious look at Lavender, but the younger girl, although pale, appeared composed. She bent to put her circlet of berries and winter green on the dark earth.

'There!' She stood back. 'I miss father so much, you know, Caroline! It is odd, for we spoke little and then not on matters of any great import, but I knew that if I ever needed his help, he would be there. He was a good man.' She sighed.

'I am sure that your brother can perform such an

office for you now,' Caroline urged, anxious to comfort. 'He has the same integrity.'

There was a pause. Lavender's blue eyes searched Caroline's face. Her own was troubled. 'I am sure that you are correct, Caroline, but it is not so easy…' She did not need to mention Julia's name again but it hung in the air between them. Then Lavender brushed the stray soil from her gloves and turned away.

'I think that father would have liked you,' she said conversationally. 'He always admired spirit!'

Caroline laughed, despite herself. 'I am scarcely spirited, Lavender! A governess cannot afford such luxuries of temperament! I must efface myself and creep about, quiet as a mouse!'

Now it was Lavender's turn to laugh. She wrinkled up her nose. 'Fustian to that, Caroline! What could be more spirited than having to go out into the world and earn a living? I do not mean spirit in the sense of wilfulness, but I believe you have true courage!'

Caroline was touched and sought to turn attention away from herself. 'I wonder how the Marchioness of Sywell fares, poor creature!' she said lightly. 'She must have had a strange time of it, with no friends either before or after her marriage—'

'Oh, Louise had a friend—' Lavender began, then broke off, the colour rushing into her face. Caroline watched in puzzlement, wondering if Lavender had been about to imply that the Marchioness had run away with a man, but after a moment, Lavender said, in a rush, 'It's just that I saw her several times speaking to Athene Filmer, who lives with her mother in

Steep Ride. I believe they were firm friends.' She shot
Caroline a shamefaced look. 'There has always been
much gossip about Louise Hanslope, I believe, but I
never gave it credence! To suggest that she was the
bailiff's natural daughter was quite foolish and the
tales going about now are even worse! I hate that sort
of spite!' She took a deep breath. 'Oh, I am sorry,
Caroline! I am sure you were not expecting a sermon
from me!'

Caroline was intrigued and a little amused at
Lavender's defence of the mysterious Louise. Perhaps
it was that Lavender felt that both she and Louise
were different, neither fitting comfortably into a con-
ventional society. Certainly, Caroline could see that
Lavender, with her honesty and lack of artifice, would
find hurtful gossip to be nothing but malicious. The
thought inevitably made Caroline see how difficult it
would be for Lavender to live with Julia for any
length of time, and they both made their way back to
the lychgate with slow steps.

It was dusk by the time Caroline left Lavender at
Perceval Hall, with her friend promising to return to
Hewly within the week. Lady Perceval pressed her to
take the carriage home, remarking that the January
afternoons were short and that darkness could come
up very quickly. Caroline thanked her and reassured
her that there was plenty of time, and armed with a
basket full of eggs, fresh churned butter and a loaf of
bread that was still warm, she started to make her way
back to Hewly through the twilight.

The moon was climbing up through the trees and

Caroline drew her cloak closer about her. It was cold, far colder than it had been the previous night, and she thought that predictions of another snowfall could well be true. She began to wish that she had accepted the carriage after all. It was dark under the trees, and although she had strong nerves Caroline jumped a little at the strange rustlings of the undergrowth. She knew that she was almost back at the Hewly estate, but when she saw the flicker of faint lights in the woods up ahead, she froze in near panic. The lights dodged between the trees, glimmering in the darkness as though in some unearthly dance. Caroline inconveniently began to remember all the folk stories she had read about the countryside round and about the Manor, the tales of spirits in the woods, the story of the grey lady…

Abruptly she turned and plunged through the undergrowth, seeking the edge of the wood, and resolved to run across the open fields if she had to. She had barely gone thirty yards when the trees ended and she found herself on a rough track beside a high hawthorn hedge. Panting a little, she leant against a field gate to get her breath back, and jumped a mile when an unmistakable voice said, 'I had no idea that you favoured such strenuous exercise, Miss Whiston! Dashing about in the woods at dusk! You are fortunate that I did not shoot you by accident!'

'Captain Brabant!' Caroline drew herself up and tried to catch her breath. She was not sure whether she was glad or annoyed to be caught out in such a situation. 'Shooting in the dark does not sound a very sensible occupation!'

Lewis Brabant laughed. He let himself through the gate and stood beside her, his shotgun across his arm. 'Do you seek to reproach me, Miss Whiston? Running around on your own is an even less sensible occupation and certainly not an appropriate one!'

'I thought I saw some lights in the wood—' Caroline began, to break off as Lewis's hand closed firmly about her wrist.

'Miss Whiston, come closer to me—'

'What on earth—' Caroline stopped as he drew her deep into the shelter of the hedge. The sharp spikes of hawthorn prickled through her cloak, but still he pulled her deeper into the shadow. And then there was a step on the road, the sound of muffled voices, the rustle of leaves as the wind passed by, and they were left in silence once more.

Caroline realised that she had been holding her breath. She noticed in the same moment that she was pressed against the whole length of Lewis's body, and stepped away hastily. 'What…who…what was that?'

'Poachers,' Lewis said softly, unlatching the gate with the softest of clicks. 'This way, Miss Whiston, and quickly. You can only just have missed them.'

He took her hand and pulled her quickly across the field, so that Caroline was almost running again in the effort to keep up. It was only when they reached a stile on the opposite side and tumbled down into the road that ran by the school that he allowed his pace to slacken.

'I don't understand,' Caroline said, a little breath-lessly, as she followed Lewis through the gateway into the Manor stable yard. 'You had a gun—surely if you had challenged them—'

Lewis gave her a look that silenced her. His voice was low and angry. 'Do you think that I would have dreamed of challenging a gang of poachers when I had you to protect, Miss Whiston? Of all the fool-hardy actions… Please consider what might have hap-pened if you had stumbled on them alone during your wanderings in the wood, and promise me that you will not indulge in such reckless behaviour again!'

Caroline knew that he was right but for some rea-son it grated on her to admit it. 'I am not reckless! I always behave appropriately—'

Lewis flashed her a look of mingled irritation and contempt. 'Oh, spare me the denials! You have no more idea how to go on than an infant in arms! The truth is that you are so bored with your circumscribed life that you get into danger through most unseemly behaviour!'

Caroline glared at him, furious now. 'How dare you so criticise me, sir! At least I have the good manners to know that it is not fitting to argue in public!'

'Then let us step inside,' Lewis said with biting sarcasm, 'so that I may quarrel with you in private! Your conduct is not only improper, Miss Whiston, but downright dangerous—'

One of the stable doors opened and a groom came out into the yard. Caroline bit back an angry retort and waited whilst Lewis handed the gun over and exchanged a few words. She toyed with the idea of leaving him there and stalking off into the house, but there was something in Lewis's demeanour that suggested he would probably deal with her in a summary and unbecoming manner were she to do so.

'I see that Mrs Chessford and Captain Slater have returned,' she said tightly, nodding towards the carriage that was standing waiting to be put away. 'At least we may have some congenial company at dinner!'

'I will allow you to exchange my unwelcome presence for Richard's more agreeable company shortly,' Lewis said, as stiffly as she, 'but not until I have your promise, Miss Whiston. You are too precipitate. You will not go wandering off alone again—'

Caroline felt as though she was going to burst with anger. She started to walk away towards the house. Lewis caught her arm.

'Miss Whiston!'

Caroline was appalled to find that there were tears in her eyes. She had no idea how they could have reached such a pitch of conflict. She had spent her working life soothing the sensibilities of others and it should have been easy to efface herself, give her word, dismiss the quarrel as unimportant. Yet as she looked up into Lewis's angry face, all she wanted to do was to hurt him.

'You are not my employer, to constrain me so—'

Lewis's brows snapped together. 'No, I am not, as you were so good to remind me once before! Yet I must also remind you, Miss Whiston, that Hewly is my house and whilst you are under my roof you will submit to my instructions! Now, your word—'

'Oh, you have it, sir!' Caroline snatched her arm from his grasp. 'Though why it could possibly matter—' She felt a sob rise in her throat and broke off. 'And you need have no fear for my safety! Once I am gone from Hewly I shall be no more of your concern!'

She turned on her heel and walked off, and though she did not look back, she had the disconcerting feeling that Lewis was watching her all the way to the house.

It was largely due to Richard Slater's presence that dinner was so pleasant an experience. Caroline had been dreading having to face Lewis again, but she found that he was perfectly civil to her. His manner was distant and he allowed Julia to monopolise his attention, suggesting to Caroline that he had already dismissed their quarrel from his mind. Richard, by contrast, gave her an amusing summary of the trip to Northampton, asked her opinion on the Luddite riots that were causing so much trouble in towns and cities further north, and engaged her in a lively debate on the merits of the poems of Samuel Taylor Coleridge.

'Lud, poetry!' Julia yawned, when the discussion had finally come to a close. 'What a pity Lavender is not here to converse with you both! She is a frighteningly accomplished young woman!' She smiled at Lewis. ''Tis a shame we cannot have any music, though I suppose with dear Uncle Harley so recently passed on... When do you expect Churchward to be here for the reading of the will, Lewis?'

'In a few days, I imagine.' Lewis reached over to pull the bell. 'He writes that he has been delayed by the unfortunate death of Lord Nantwich.'

'Oh yes,' Julia looked animated. 'Did he not die in a carriage accident with his mistress, whilst on the way to visit the family of his affianced bride? The *on dit* is that he had intended to install the woman in a local hostelry and visit her every evening! Why, did you know that...'

Caroline turned away and closed her ears to the gossip. It was an interesting fact that Julia had often declared herself to have forgotten everything she had ever learned at Mrs Guarding's school, yet she maintained an encyclopedic knowledge of scandal.

They all retired early. Julia declared herself fatigued by the journey from Northampton, then insisted on having Caroline's company in her room and chattered endlessly about Lewis and Richard Slater and which of them was the better prospect.

'For though Lewis is better-looking, Richard is more gallant! I find that Lewis has an odd, ironical way with him sometimes! But then there is the estate, for Lewis is quite a rich man, you know, and I have not been able to ascertain Richard's fortune...'

Caroline had a decided headache by the time that she escaped to her bedroom. She sat down on the bed with a sigh and rubbed her aching temples. The room looked very cosy, with the fire burning bright and the candlelight concealing the worn patches in the rugs and curtains. There had been none of Julia's home improvements here. Caroline reached up to unpin her hair, and at the same moment her eye caught a scrap of white protruding from under the bed. She bent down curiously and saw that it was the corner of a letter.

Dropping to her knees, Caroline lifted the bed-spread and pulled out the old trunk that contained her keepsakes and letters. Her grandfather's watch was still there, as was the locket left to her by her mother and the other little bits and pieces she had accumulated over the years. But there was nothing else. Where previously there had been bundles of letters tied with ribbon, now there was an empty space. Julia's letters to her had all disappeared.

Caroline stared in disbelief and mounting anger, going down on her knees again and peering under the bed. There was no mistake. All the letters had vanished. She sat back on her heels and surveyed the room for signs of disturbance, but there were none. That, and the fact that the letters were all that was missing, suggested that the thief had known exactly what he was looking for.

Caroline got to her feet slowly. She did not wish to believe it, but there could be very little doubt that it was Lewis Brabant who had stolen them, and as she thought about it her fury started to grow. Lewis was the only one who knew about the letters, for he had found the one in the book and quizzed her about it. Then he had asked her about them again, only a few days ago. She had refused to discuss Julia's correspondence and had foolishly believed that he had accepted her decision, but it seemed not, and now she would have to confront him about it…

Caroline glanced at the clock and acknowledged that it would be the height of folly to beard Lewis in his room at this hour. The last time she had encountered him late at night, the consequences had been extreme. The matter would have to wait until the morning.

Unfortunately that gave her too long to dwell on the situation. She tossed and turned all night, and by the time the morning came she was equally full of apprehension and anger. She knew that she did not look her best, for her face was drawn from both strain and lack of sleep, and she would have done anything to put off the confrontation. However, she knew it would not serve. She had to see Lewis at once.

She found him in the library, apparently discussing horseflesh with Richard Slater. Captain Slater took one look at Caroline's face and made a hasty excuse.

'Well, I shall go directly to the stables and see what I think, Lewis. Perhaps you will join me later. Good morning, Miss Whiston…'

Alone with Lewis in the unnerving silence, Caroline found her apprehension growing rather than diminishing. Lewis gave her a cool smile that reminded her of their previous quarrel and Caroline's heart sank even further. This was going to be very difficult.

'Well, Miss Whiston? What can I do for you?'

'I have come to ask you to give me my letters back,' Caroline said, in a rush. She could feel the colour rising to her face. 'I must insist, Captain—they are my property and should never have been taken!'

Lewis' smile was fading. 'I beg your pardon, Miss Whiston? To what do you refer?'

'You know full well!' Caroline's overstretched nerves found relief in anger. 'You know that I kept all of Julia's letters over the years—you saw one yourself! Do you deny it?'

'Of course I do not deny it,' Lewis said reasonably, frowning a little. 'Forgive me, Miss Whiston, but I fear I am confused. What has happened to the letters?'

'Oh, do not seek to gammon me!' Caroline snapped. 'The letters have been stolen! I refused to tell you about their contents so you took them yourself! It is obvious who is the culprit!'

There was a silence, but for the ticking of the long-case clock. Lewis' eyes had narrowed. He rested both hands flat on the table and leaned towards her. His voice was very level. 'A moment, Miss Whiston. Do I understand that you are accusing me of theft?'

'What other explanation is there?' Caroline stared at him. 'You were the only one who knew about the letters! You asked me about their contents and I refused to tell you! So—'

'So you think that I went creeping about my own home to wrest from you that which you would not give willingly?' Lewis straightened up and drove his hands into his jacket pockets. With a queer jump of the heart, Caroline realised that he was very angry and that this was different from their quarrel the previous day. He was looking at her with disgust.

Caroline backed away, feeling suddenly intimidated, but Lewis reached her side in two strides and put his hand out.

'Do not hurry away, Miss Whiston! We have not finished discussing this yet!' He pulled her around to face him, his blue eyes hard with dislike. 'We had just reached the interesting subject of your opinion of me! Unscrupulous, devious and a thief, I infer!'

'I...' Caroline faltered. It had not occurred to her previously that she might have made a mistake. It had seemed so obvious; Lewis had wanted the letters, the letters had disappeared and therefore he must have taken them. Part of her anger, she realised now, had sprung from her disappointment in him. She had believed him principled and honourable, only to find that he had stooped to subterfuge and stealing. Or so she had thought. She had acted impulsively, and now it seemed that she might have made a dreadful error...

'I will not waste my time in protesting my innocence,' Lewis was saying coldly. 'If that is your opinion—'

'What else was I to think?' Caroline asked desperately, stepping back and spreading her hands in a gesture of despair. 'You wanted those letters—and they have gone! Someone must have taken them!'

For a long moment Lewis stared down into her face. 'Not merely anyone, Miss Whiston! You believed that I, myself...' He broke off, shaking his head. 'Well, I would restore your letters to you if I had them, but I fear I do not!'

He turned away and strode across the room. Caroline hurried after him.

'I am sorry if I have made a mistake.' She put her hand tentatively on his arm and felt the tense anger in him. She was only slightly encouraged that he did not immediately shake her off. 'I will not seek to make excuses. It was wrong of me to doubt you—'

Lewis turned to look at her. The coldness and dislike were still plain in his eyes. 'Pray do not apologise, Miss Whiston! I thought I had your good opinion, but it seems I was mistaken! Now, I have business to attend to. Good day to you!'

And he went out, leaving the air still humming with his anger.

Chapter Nine

Mr Churchward, of the eminent London lawyers of the same name, arrived that same evening, just before dusk. Lewis sent a messenger to Perceval Hall to acquaint Lavender with the news, and the official reading of the will was set to take place the following morning.

In the meantime, Mr Churchward requested a few private words and Lewis steered him into the study to take a glass of port. If the news of his inheritance was bad, he felt that the lawyer would probably need a stiff drink even more than he would.

They settled in the wing chairs before the fire, but Lewis had noted at once that the lawyer could not be content with small talk, for he fidgeted with the clasp of his document case and rustled his papers at frequent intervals. Recognising these signs of agitation, Lewis decided to cut to the chase.

'Well, Churchward, it seems there are certain matters causing you concern. Would you care to enlighten me?'

The lawyer cleared his throat portentously. 'Thank you, Captain Brabant. There are a number of issues that are a trifle irregular…'

Lewis passed him a glass of port and raised an eyebrow expectantly. 'Yes, Churchward? I must say that you do surprise me. Of all the things my father was, *irregular* could hardly be described as one of them…'

Mr Churchward regarded him with mournful eyes. 'One never can tell, Captain.' He shook his head slowly. 'It is not that the Admiral's affairs are not in order, simply that some of his requests are somewhat quixotic…'

Lewis smiled ruefully. 'It is a character trait I share, sir. Pray do not spare me—let us get straight to business. What are these irregular conditions to which you refer?'

Mr Churchward cleared his throat again and extracted a sheet of paper from the pile. He placed his glasses on the end of his nose. 'Well, sir. The Admiral's will is relatively straightforward, given the fact that the estate is not entailed and there are only a small number of beneficiaries. He altered his will after the untimely death of your brother, of course.'

Churchward paused for a suitably respectful moment.

Lewis nodded briskly. 'Understood, Churchward.'

'You are to inherit the estate of Hewly and the bulk of the Admiral's fortune,' Churchward continued. He gave a small, dry smile. 'The Admiral has made some sound investments over the years, sir. You are to be congratulated.'

Lewis inclined his head. 'Thank you, Churchward. Fortune has favoured the Brabant family, although fate has exacted a high cost with my brother's death.'

Mr Churchward assumed an expression of dolefulness. 'Indeed, sir. The inheritance is not entirely straightforward, however. It is contingent upon two facts, but it is perhaps preferable that we deal with other matters before coming to those. Now, there are the usual bequests to servants and retainers, of course, and two additional beneficiaries.'

'My sister and my father's ward?'

'Precisely so.' Again a hint of uneasiness seemed to enter Churchward's demeanour. He had not touched his port. Lewis noted his discomfiture and wondered. He leant back in his chair and waited in silence.

'Your sister Miss Lavender Brabant is given a dowry of ten thousand pounds. If she has not married by the age of twenty-five the money reverts to her absolutely.'

Lewis raised his brows. 'Very enlightened of my father! There are no other stipulations attached?'

'None whatsoever, sir.' Churchward shuffled his papers again, then looked him straight in the eye. 'Now your father's ward, Mrs Chessford. She inherits the sum of one thousand pounds.'

Lewis pursed his lips in a soundless whistle. That was scarcely enough to keep Julia in the style to which she aspired and he knew she would be deeply disappointed. The Admiral had been both godfather and guardian to her and he was a rich man. She could justifiably have expected more. Lewis shifted a little uncomfortably, remembering the unpalatable story that Julia had told him about his father's behaviour. If the Admiral had proposed to Julia and she had rejected him, this looked very much like a spiteful revenge…

'The bequest is smaller than I had anticipated,' he said carefully. 'Did my father give any reason why he should leave his ward so small a legacy?'

Mr Churchward fidgeted a little. He was looking at his most dry and formal, an expression which gave Lewis to think that even had the Admiral explained at great length, his lawyer was not about to share that with him.

'No, Captain, not precisely. I believe,' Mr Churchward wetted his lips with the port, 'that he felt that Mrs Chessford had a large enough fortune of her own. That is, she did before—' Mr Churchward made a vague gesture and Lewis understood what he meant. Julia had had a substantial fortune of her own before she and Jack Chessford had squandered it about Town. Lewis had heard the rumours and perhaps his father had too.

'I had mentioned that the Admiral changed his will in your favour after your brother's death,' Churchward said dryly. 'It was at this time that he also made a change to Mrs Chessford's legacy. Before that the figure had been…ah…considerably larger.'

Lewis sighed and rested his chin on his hand. The

difficulty was that all actions were open to interpretation when one of the parties was dead and could not therefore state his side of the case. The Admiral had disapproved of Julia's behaviour for one reason or another... Lewis became aware that Churchward's eyes were fixed on his face in the manner of one who has some further, even less appealing news to relate.

'The two contingencies, sir...' The lawyer murmured.

'Oh, of course.' Lewis drained his glass of port and sat back. 'My inheritance is dependent upon two factors. Pray tell me, Mr Churchward...'

Churchward looked gratified at this businesslike request.

'Of course, sir. Your father made the following stipulations. Firstly that you should marry within a twelvemonth of coming into the estate. The Admiral said—' He cleared his throat and quoted: 'There should be no long faces and foolish fussing over mourning. The boy—yourself, I believe, sir—should settle down, marry and produce an heir...'

Churchward broke off at Lewis's crack of laughter.

'I suppose I should just be grateful that my father did not make the inheritance contingent upon the heir as well! Or was that his second criterion?'

'No, sir,' the lawyer said primly. 'The Admiral specified marriage within the year but the heir was—'

'An additional benefit rather than a requirement? Thank you, father!' Lewis raised his glass in mocking toast. 'So, the second stipulation...'

'Was that you should *not* marry your father's ward,

Mrs Chessford,' the lawyer finished. 'In point of fact, the Admiral stated that he could not prevent such a marriage, but if you should do so, the estate would be forfeit and would pass to your sister.'

This time there was a silence. Lewis refilled his glass, taking his time. 'But that is outrageous,' he said quietly, after a moment. 'If I wish to marry Julia—'

'You will lose your inheritance. Yes, Captain, that is precisely the case.'

Lewis ran a hand through his hair. 'But why—'

Mr Churchward had assumed his favourite sympathetic expression, the one reserved for the breaking of bad news.

'I am sorry, sir. Your father was most insistent.'

'And he gave no reason?'

'No, indeed. He gave no reason at all.'

Lewis raised his head. 'I see. Then there is no more to be said, Mr Churchward. You will, of course, be obliged to disclose all of these facts tomorrow?'

The lawyer nodded slowly. 'I will, Captain. You will understand now why I wished you to be apprised of them in advance?'

Lewis nodded absently. 'Yes, Churchward, I thank you for the warning.' He stood up. 'I need some time to think. Now do you care to join the others, sir, or would you prefer to retire? After your long journey…'

The lawyer took the hint. 'Yes, Captain,' he said quietly, 'I think that would be for the best.'

'How could he be so cruel!' Julia wailed piteously, shredding her delicate handkerchief to strips and fix-

ing Caroline with her desolate blue eyes. 'Why, I
cared for Uncle Harley like a daughter and how does
he repay me? By leaving me next to nothing and sep-
arating me from the only man I ever loved!'

Caroline reflected that it was the first time she had
ever seen Julia cry real tears. At school Julia had always been able to cry on order if she needed to render
a teacher more sympathetic, but she was seldom genuinely upset. Now, of course, she had been denied the
two things she wanted most in the world and two
huge drops were rolling down her cheeks towards her
quivering lips. She dabbed at them ineffectually.

'It is so unjust of him! The money is bad enough—
how shall I manage now!—but to be torn apart from
Lewis is too cruel!' She peeked at Caroline. 'We had
talked a little of the future and both of us knew how
we wished it to be. Oh, of course, Lewis could make
no formal declaration, with Uncle Harley's death and
matters so uncertain, but now!' She gave a sob. 'We
have waited so long, and now it is never to be!'

'Perhaps Captain Brabant will disregard his father's
wishes if his feelings are so strong,' Caroline said,
feeling the words stick in her throat. She had no wish
to dwell on the thought, but it seemed possible that
Lewis would renounce his inheritance for Julia if he
truly loved her. He was not the man to be dictated to
or to be tied by worldly considerations. 'Besides, the
Captain has his own fortune and need not be dependent on his inheritance—'

'Oh…' Julia sighed heavily. 'I could not ask Lewis
to make such a sacrifice. To choose between his love

and his duty—no man should be so obliged! Besides, Lewis has money of his own but it is nothing compared to the Hewly estate and fortune! He would be obliged to work for a living!' She wrinkled up her nose. 'Oh, how dreadful! No, I have decided that I shall go away! It is the only solution!' She caught Caroline's sleeve. 'Dearest Caro, you will come with me, shall you not? We shall live in a cottage together and it shall be delightful…'

Caroline could think of little that was less appealing. To hear Julia bemoaning her lack of funds when a thousand pounds was more than she could earn in a lifetime was particularly galling.

'I have to earn a living, Julia…' she temporised, 'and I doubt that you could bear the expense of a companion now—'

Julia patted her hand. 'Well, but I have a little to share! And we are *friends*… My mind is made up! We shall leave Hewly in a few days' time! Now—' she cast her handkerchief aside '—pray send Letty to me, for I must organise my portmanteaux! I will call you in a little, Caroline, to write my letters for me!'

Caroline went downstairs to find that Lavender was just bidding farewell to Mr Churchward. She turned with relief as Caroline came up and closed the heavy outside door.

'Caroline! Thank goodness! Will you take tea with me? I need someone to talk to!' She looked closely at Caroline's face. 'Dear me, perhaps you need a confidante too!'

They settled in the drawing-room with Lavender presiding over the silver pot.

'Lewis and Captain Slater have gone out for a ride,' Lavender said, stirring the tea. 'Poor Lewis, I think he wished to escape for a little! And really, it is monstrous of father to have behaved so, though I cannot but be glad!' She poured tea daintily into the two china cups. 'I confess myself puzzled, however. Why should father do such a thing? I know he did not approve of Julia hanging out for Andrew, but that is scarcely enough…' Her voice trailed away in puzzlement.

Caroline had been wondering this very fact herself. She was not missish, and had even speculated that Julia could be the Admiral's natural daughter and therefore Lewis's half-sister, which would of course have precluded a match. However, she had seen a locket of Julia's with a picture of her father in it, and the fair good looks of the Beechams were unmistakable in father and daughter. There could be no family reason to forbid the banns, so there had to be some other barrier. But Julia, even in her most impassioned railing against the Admiral's decisions, had not identified a reason…

'Lewis was asking me this morning whether it was true that Papa was set against Julia marrying Andrew,' Lavender said, still frowning. 'Then he asked me what happened the night Julia arrived here three months ago! I tried to answer as best I could but I do so dislike mysteries! Still,' her brow lightened a little, 'there is one matter that need concern me no longer! Is it very bad of me, Caroline, to be so pleased that I will not have Julia as a sister-in-law?'

Caroline tried not to smile. 'My dear Lavender! Have you yet considered the possibility that your brother might renounce his inheritance for Julia? Then you would be heiress to Hewly and have Julia as a sister into the bargain!'

Lavender clapped her hand to her mouth, but quickly recovered herself. 'Oh no! But I should not at all wish to be the owner of Hewly! No, Lewis will never give up the estate for Julia!'

'He may put love before duty,' Caroline said, feeling as though she had to point out the possibility even though it wrenched at her own heart.

'No,' Lavender said again, apparently restored to serenity, 'Lewis does not care enough for Julia to do such a thing! In fact,' she raised her lavender-coloured eyes to Caroline's face, 'I do not believe that he cares for her at all! He must look elsewhere for a bride!'

Caroline felt herself blush under her friend's penetrating scrutiny. 'Well, there are plenty of other eligible young ladies in the neighbourhood, and he has a whole twelvemonth—'

'Pooh, Caroline, do not be so foolish!' Lavender smiled at her. 'You would be perfect for Lewis! And I know he likes you! What could be better?'

Caroline reddened even more. 'You mistake, Lavender. Your brother and I would not suit! Besides,

I am scarce eligible! Anyway, I am to go away. Julia plans to leave Hewly in a few days—'

'Well, you need not go too!' Lavender leant forward urgently. 'Please, Caroline, stay here with me instead! I could do with a companion!'

Caroline shook her head. 'Lavender, I cannot. I have written away for other posts—'

'Because of Julia? But you need not worry, for if you stay here with me—'

'It is not just that.' Caroline spoke desperately. She put her cup down. 'There are other reasons—'

'It is because of Lewis, isn't it!' Lavender sat back with some satisfaction. 'I knew it! I knew you cared for him!'

Caroline put both her hands up to her burning cheeks. 'Oh Lavender, pray do not!'

'I'm sorry!' The younger girl looked suddenly upset. 'Dear Caroline, I will not press you to stay if you do not wish it, nor will I embarrass you any further. But,' she hesitated, 'please do not go with Julia! If you must take another post, stay here until it can be arranged! I promise—'

A bell rang from within the depths of the house. 'That will be Julia,' Caroline said evenly. 'She wishes me to write her some letters—'

'Oh, why can she not write for herself!' Lavender said stormily. She sounded more agitated than Caroline had ever heard her. She stood up, almost sending the tea-tray crashing to the floor. 'Oh, it puts me out of all patience to see you at her beck and call!

It is simply not right! I am going to visit Nanny Prior! She will know what to do for the best!'

Caroline sighed as she righted the tea-table and tidied up the cups. Matters suddenly seemed very uncertain. She would dearly have loved to stay at Hewly with Lavender, who was the best of good friends. Her feelings for Lewis precluded such a course of action, however. Then there was Julia, who might still become the next Mrs Brabant were Lewis to renounce his inheritance. Whatever the outcome, her role as Julia's companion had to come to an end.

The bell rang again, impatiently. Caroline smoothed her gown. She knew that the only outcome was to take up another post, away from Julia, Lavender, and Lewis most of all. It was a sensible course of action. It was appropriate. And it seemed a desolate future.

Later, after Julia had dictated so many letters that Caroline's hand positively ached, she finally escaped to the library for a little solitude. It was not yet time for dinner but the lamps were lit and the January evening was drawing in. Feeling strangely restless, Caroline drew near to the fire and stood for a while looking into its glowing heart. She heard Lewis and Richard Slater come in from their ride, and tensed as she waited to see if they would come into the library.

Since her quarrel with Lewis the previous day there had been no time to ask for forgiveness and Caroline doubted that he would accept her apology anyway. Not that it mattered—Lewis had far greater issues to consider than a foolish argument with Julia's companion! Caroline shrank a little at her own presumption in imagining that he would even remember it and resolved that it would be better simply to avoid him until she left.

The voices faded away and Caroline sighed a little and moved over to the bookshelves, looking for something to distract her mind. The books by the writer of *Sense and Sensibility* were not so appealing at a time like this, mirroring as cleverly as it did the trials of everyday life. Instead Caroline's eye was caught by the rows of old estate maps, and she remembered what Lewis had said about the garden designs dating back to the time of the Percevals. It might distract her a little to study the old plans.

She put out a hand and pulled one of the maps from the shelf. The paper stuck slightly, as though caught on another document, and Caroline paused so that she did not rip the old parchments. She took out two or three of the maps, found that they were all stuck together and began cautiously to separate them out.

Something fell from between the folds of one of the maps and Caroline bent down for a closer look. It was a piece of paper, folded roughly, blotched and splotched with ink. Caroline's heart began to race. She remembered Nanny Prior's words about the document the Admiral had been writing on the night he died, the one that had not been seen since and was almost forgotten. Perhaps this could be the very letter, though what it was doing amongst the estate maps was a mystery in itself. Turning the paper over in her hands, Caroline saw that it had Lewis's name at the top.

'My dear Lewis,

I am writing this in great haste lest I never have the chance to tell you—'

Guiltily, Caroline looked away and stuffed the letter into the pocket of her gown. She bundled the maps together again and pushed them haphazardly back on to the shelves, all the time frantically thinking of what she should do. There seemed to be little choice. Although it had only been five minutes previously that she had resolved to avoid Lewis for the rest of her time at Hewly, she was going to have to seek him out. There was no alternative.

She moved over to the fireplace and rang the bell, telling the footman who answered that she wished him to tell the Captain that she requested an appointment. In a surprisingly short time, the man reappeared.

'Captain Brabant's compliments, Miss Whiston, and he will see you now in the study.' The footman bowed and backed out of the room, waiting politely for Caroline to precede him into the hall. Caroline went, feeling distinctly nervous. But then, she told herself sternly, all she had to do was to hand the letter to Lewis and withdraw. Her obligation in passing him the Admiral's last message would then be fulfilled.

'Miss Whiston.' Lewis stood up as she came into the room and waited until the servant had closed the door behind her. His expression was unreadable. 'You wished to speak with me, ma'am?'

'Yes, I...' Caroline cursed herself for her inarticulateness. All her eloquence seemed to have deserted her of late whenever she was near him. She could not believe that she could be so tongue-tied. She came forward hesitantly and held out the letter.

'I found this today, sir—just now—and felt that it should be handed to you immediately. Now if you will excuse me—'

'Please take a seat.' Caroline could not be sure whether Lewis was so preoccupied that he had not heard her, or was simply ignoring her plea to escape. His head was bent over the letter and he did not look at her, but his words seemed unequivocal enough. She sat down gingerly on the edge of one of the chairs and waited whilst he started to read.

'This is in my father's hand,' Lewis said, looking up suddenly. 'You say that you found it recently, Miss Whiston?'

'It was in one of the old estate maps.' Caroline felt uncomfortable, as though she had been prying. 'I was not certain whether or not it was important, sir—for all I know it may be several years old, but as it was addressed to you—'

'Did you read it?' Lewis asked sharply.

Caroline coloured a little.

'Only to find the direction, sir...'

She saw Lewis's mouth twist in a slight smile at her use of the same words he had once spoken to her.

'I see.' He scanned the rest of the letter quickly. 'So you have no notion of the contents?'

'Not in the least, sir.' Caroline held his gaze. 'As

I have said, I do not even know if it is a recent letter or several years of age. The only reason I thought it might be important was that I remembered Mrs Prior saying that the Admiral was writing a letter when he was taken ill. So I wondered...'

'If this was that very letter?' Lewis was watching her intently. 'Did Mrs Prior say that? I had not heard that tale. But then, there is much that I have not heard...'

Caroline frowned a little, uncertain what he meant. Lewis smiled. 'Forgive me for the mystery. But this is odd. There seem to be too many missing letters in this house! Do I take it that you have not found yours?'

Caroline blushed. 'No, indeed, sir. I have searched everywhere.' She got to her feet. She knew she had to apologise and she felt better standing up. 'Captain Brabant, I feel I should—'

'Please, Miss Whiston,' Lewis held his hand up, 'if you are about to refer to our disagreement then I beg you do not.'

'But—' Caroline watched as he crossed the room towards her. Somehow his approach made her feel vulnerable. She toyed with the idea of sitting down again and changed her mind. That would be even worse.

'You must permit me, sir... That is, I wished to apologise...'

Lewis came right up to her. Caroline looked up into his face and completely lost the thread of what she had been saying. There was a smile in the blue eyes that told her more eloquently than any words that she was forgiven. She tore her gaze away from his and realised with horror that her hand was now resting against his chest. She withdrew it hastily.

'Your apology is accepted, ma'am,' Lewis said gently. 'We have both made errors of judgement.' He gave her a smile that sent the blood tingling through Caroline's veins. 'Let us study to do better in the future.'

'I fear that there will be little time,' Caroline said, backing away from him. 'Mrs Chessford and I are to leave for London in a couple of days—' She broke off, remembering that Julia's circumstances might change again should Lewis declare himself.

'Yes, I met Lavender earlier and she told me that you planned to leave Hewly,' Lewis said. He was still watching her. 'Can we not prevail upon you to stay here, ma'am? I know that my sister would be pleased for you to stay, not as a companion, but as a guest—'

'You are both very kind,' Caroline said guardedly, avoiding his eyes, 'but I fear I cannot accept.'

'May I not press you to do so, Miss Whiston?' Lewis had taken her hand now, the pressure of his fingers insistent on hers. 'It would be more comfortable for you to remain here, even if it were only until you took up a new position—'

Caroline's misery threatened to overwhelm her. To have Lewis ask her to stay for all the wrong reasons was particularly disheartening.

'My mind is made up, I fear, sir,' she said, giving

him a tight smile. 'You really must forgive me. I cannot stay at Hewly.' She tried to free herself.

'If it is because of Julia—' Lewis began.

'Please—' Caroline found that her composure was at breaking point. 'I wish the two of you very happy, but I cannot—' She broke off before she could give herself away any further.

'Excuse me, sir,' she said. 'I must go.' And she hurried from the room before Lewis could ask any more difficult questions.

The snow started that night. It brushed against the windows, falling softly, cloaking the woodland in white. Caroline stood by her bedroom window, watching the flakes swirl in the wind and shivering a little to think of the dark night in the cold forest. The same feeling of restlessness possessed her that her dogged her footsteps all day. It was odd; she felt as though the house was waiting for something to happen. She shrugged off the fanciful notion, but even so, she found she was not tired enough to go to sleep.

The clock had struck one when Caroline heard the creak of a step on the landing outside her door. It seemed an odd time to be prowling about, and she wondered whether Lavender was unable to sleep and was needing some company. She opened her door softly. The dark stairs stretched away below and Caroline could just see an insubstantial figure descending into the gloom. Then a stair creaked sharply. Caroline froze. What kind of spectre was it that trod so heavily that the ground shook beneath their feet? Perhaps the sort who had taken her letters?

Caroline slipped out of her room and closed the door soundlessly behind her. All the doors leading off the landing and the corridor beyond were closed and blank. She paused for a moment. There was a sound from below—the noise of a step on stone. The air shivered a little with the draught of an opening door. Intrigued now, Caroline crept down the stairs. The hall was all in darkness, which made navigation difficult, but Caroline thought that she espied a flickering light moving behind the door of the servants' quarters. She hesitated, unsure whether to go in and confront whoever was lurking there, or to wait and see if they emerged again. Whatever they were up to was evidently secret, for the light glimmered erratically and there was no sound.

Caroline put her hand on the door knob and was about to turn it when a sudden sound from further down the corridor made her jump almost out of her skin. Someone was coming out of the study; a different person from the one whose light she could still see behind the closed door, but someone equally secretive and cautious. Without further thought, Caroline dived through the open door on her left. It was the library.

The curtains were not drawn and the sharp moonlight reflected on the snow outside and lit the room with a bright white glow. Without conscious thought, Caroline made for the window and pulled the heavy velvet curtain about her. She thought that she could hear pursuing footsteps on the stone flags of the hall, and suddenly it seemed foolish in the extreme to be creeping about in the dark, particularly without anything with which to protect herself. She was about to emerge into the room to arm herself with a candlestick when there was a sound on the threshold and the door closed with a slight but unmistakable click.

They were in the room with her. Although Caroline could hear nothing, some sixth sense told her that she was no longer alone. She froze as still as a mouse, yet she was certain that whoever it was who was standing inside the door, watching and waiting, could hear her frightened breathing. Telling herself that there could be no danger, that she was no silly girl to be frightened by gothic horrors, Caroline drew herself up to her full height. In a moment, when she had steadied her nerves, she would throw back the curtain and confront whoever was there…

Even as the thought went through her head, the curtain was seized and thrown back, and she found herself looking into the furious features of Lewis Brabant.

Chapter Ten

'What the hell...' Lewis began angrily. He cut off whatever he was about to say and ran a hand through his hair, as though the gesture could help dissipate some of his pent-up fury.

'What the devil are you doing here, Caroline?'

'What am I doing here!' Caroline exclaimed. 'What are *you* doing, scaring me half out of my wits—'

Someone else moved in the shadows and Caroline smothered a squeak of alarm. Lewis clapped a hand over her mouth. 'Quiet! It's only Richard—'

Captain Slater came forward into the moonlight. He sketched an immaculate bow. 'Servant, Miss Whiston.'

Caroline stifled a ridiculous desire to laugh. Here they all were in the darkness of the library in the dead of night, whispering lines like characters in a bad play.

'What were you doing in the servants' quarters earlier?' she whispered urgently. 'I saw you—'

'That wasn't us,' Lewis began, only to break off as Richard put a hand on his arm.

'Don't believe we've time for explanations now, old chap! They're coming…'

There was a sudden noise outside the door. The effect on the men was instantaneous. Lewis stepped back behind the curtain next to Caroline, and Richard Slater moved swiftly across to the other side of the bay window, where he took up a similar stance. It was not a moment too soon. The door of the library opened and candlelight spilled into the room.

'Come along, you foolish girl!'

Caroline heard the edgy whisper as she watched through a crack in the curtains. There was no mistaking those impatient tones.

'We don't have much time! I only got as far as that prosy bore Shakespeare last time! Oh, was there ever such a clunch-headed idiot? Why can you not remember where you put it?'

Caroline heard the other figure mumble something under its breath, only to be cut off sharply.

'Cease this ridiculous whining, girl! We have not the time for it!'

Despite herself, Caroline found herself starting to smile. A moment later, Lewis threw back the curtain and stepped into the room.

'Good evening, Julia,' he said politely. 'Perhaps we may help you find whatever it is you are looking for?'

The maid, Letty, started screaming and it was Julia herself who gave her a sharp slap.

'Be quiet, you foolish creature! Do you wish to bring the whole house down around our ears?'

'It is a little late to worry about that,' Lewis said laconically. He and Richard Slater moved to light some of the candles, whilst Caroline drew the heavy curtains across the windows. Julia, who had been looking from one man to the other with a rather calculating expression on her face, stared at Caroline balefully.

'What is going on here? What is *she* doing here, Lewis? Surely I have not interrupted some tryst?'

Caroline met Julia's sharp blue gaze. 'I heard a noise and followed you downstairs, Julia,' she said quietly. 'I was curious to know what you were doing.'

'Is that so?' Julia scoffed. She seemed to be growing in confidence as the minutes passed, seating herself in the most comfortable chair and arranging her dress about her in precise folds. The candlelight shone on her guinea-gold curls and perfect profile, and Caroline felt a little sick. Julia was so artless, so plausible. Was it possible that she was about to make fools of them all?

Julia's gaze, amused and slightly condescending, went from Lewis' stern face to Richard Slater, who had urged the snivelling maid to take a seat and was now standing, rather ominously, by the door.

'Well, this is a cosy gathering!' Julia said sweetly, her eyes resting on Lewis's face. 'But why the long face, my dear? All I was looking for was a book to ease my sleeplessness—'

'Or, in fact, a set of estate maps,' Lewis suggested

softly. 'The set in which your bungling accomplice here—' he nodded towards Letty '—hid my father's last letter!'

The maid began to sob at once. 'I didn't do nothing wrong, sir! I just thought… They had had a quarrel, and if he had changed his will…'

'Be quiet, you fool!' Julia said venomously. She turned her gentlest smile on Lewis. 'The girl understands nothing! Dearest Lewis, let me explain this to you alone and not in front of all these people!'

Once again her disparaging gaze flicked over Caroline. 'Indeed, I cannot think why we need an audience! My servants and your best friend! Send them away and we shall set all to rights!'

Caroline went across and put an arm around the maid, who was crying in earnest now and grasped thankfully at the clean handkerchief Caroline handed her.

'I didn't do nothing wrong, miss,' she repeated miserably, 'only I couldn't remember where I'd put the letter—'

'Don't distress yourself, Letty,' Caroline soothed. 'The letter is found now, and—'

'The letter is found?' Julia swung round in her seat and glared at Caroline. 'By you, I suppose, you scheming creature! To think that I ever trusted you! Why, all the time you were planning to discredit me and we all know why!' Her poisonous glare turned from Caroline to Lewis. 'I do not know what she has told you, Lewis, but it was all self-seeking!

Insinuating herself into the family, befriending Miss Brabant—'

'That's enough, Julia!' Lewis spoke quietly, but there was a note in his voice that made Caroline jump and Julia fell silent, the colour coming into her face. Lewis continued. 'Miss Whiston found the letter and very properly brought it to me, since it bore my name. So you need not concern yourself any longer that it is lost.'

'Oh well,' Julia gave a casual little shrug. 'I was only looking for it because I remembered that Uncle Harley was writing when I saw him that night, and I thought it might be important. But I daresay it is of no consequence—'

'As it turns out, it is very important,' Lewis said, with a smile, 'though not, perhaps, in the way in which you imagine.' He crossed to the hearth and leant one arm along the mantelpiece. 'You will be relieved to know that the letter contained no change to his will.'

Caroline saw that Julia's face was a study in indecision. Clearly Lewis's words meant something to her, more than they could to Caroline herself, who was quite at sea. Instinct told her that Julia's motive for searching out the letter was not as altruistic as she liked to pretend, and the maid had effectively condemned her anyway. It seemed that Julia had thought that the Admiral had written a codicil to the will and had been trying to keep it quiet. In which case, what had prompted Admiral Brabant to take such a course of action?

Julia shrugged again, carelessly.

'Well, I am glad that the will still stands, but I am not surprised. It was only the tiniest quarrel, after all—'

'Is that so?' Lewis gave her a hard stare. 'Now that must be…the fifth time you have lied? Certainly not the first…'

Caroline gasped, but Julia gasped louder, her face suddenly bright red with outrage. 'How dare you, Lewis? Just what do you imply?'

Lewis shifted slightly. He seemed utterly unconcerned, unmoved by Julia's rage. 'Well, as you have asked me to explain, we shall start at the beginning. The first lie was the one you told me when you said that you had come to Hewly to care for my father. In fact, you arrived before he was taken ill, did you not, Julia? He was hale and hearty—at least for a few hours!'

Julia looked evasive. 'Well, what of it? I did not intend to deceive! I had every intention of staying here to care for Uncle Harley! Why, I loved him like a daughter—'

'So you professed,' Lewis said, and there was a grim note in his voice that sent a shiver down Caroline's spine. Letty heard it, too, and raised her head from the handkerchief for a moment, her eyes darting like a frightened rabbit. Richard Slater looked unmoved, his face like granite.

Julia's face was working like boiling milk. 'I do not see why I should bear this nonsense any more!' she said stormily. 'I never intended to mislead—if I forgot to tell you that Uncle Harley was well when I arrived—'

'It was because you did not wish to have to explain the cause of his sudden illness,' Lewis finished, giving her a very straight look. 'But we shall come to that. For next there was the matter of your…forced marriage…'

Caroline shot Julia an incredulous look. The letters had scarce implied any coercion, in fact Julia had been quite ruthless in setting her cap first at Andrew Brabant and then at Jack Chessford. Looking up, she caught Lewis's eye and saw the cynical gleam there.

'You may remember, Julia, that after my father died you told me a sad and affecting tale of how he had tried to force you into marriage with my brother,' Lewis said smoothly. 'When Andrew died, you told me that my father had put himself forward as a suitor in his place, so anxious was he to keep your fortune in the family. You had been so much in fear…' Lewis hesitated, 'that you chose to elope with Jack Chessford in order to escape him.'

His eyes met Caroline's for a moment, dark and sombre, and it seemed that he was speaking directly to her. 'I confess that I was horrified by the tale. A man in my father's position, a position of trust, to so abuse his ward that she felt she had to flee! It sickened me!' He sighed. 'Of course, I could not ask him if it were true, for he was beyond both recall or confession. I was the one who had to live with the horror of it.'

Julia stirred slightly in her chair. 'Well, I am sorry for it, but truth must out!'

'Indeed!' Lewis said quietly. 'And my father's will appeared to bear this out! It seemed that he had taken his rejection so badly that he wished to punish you, Julia! Not only did he leave you a smaller sum than you had hoped for, but he also expressly forbade that we should marry. He had known, of course, that I was once at your feet—' again, Lewis's gaze met Caroline's, his expression unreadable '—and no doubt he suspected that such sweet feelings might reassert themselves when we were together once more. So he asked me to choose between my inheritance and the woman I had once loved.' Lewis looked away, into the fire. 'That was one interpretation of events. There was, however, another. The true version.'

There was a silence. Even Julia was looking a little frightened now.

'The truth of it,' Lewis said softly, 'is that it was *your* desire to marry my brother, and none of my father's doing. Nor did he ever press his suit on you or make improper advances. You quarrelled with him on the night you returned to Hewly and tried to black-mail him for money. He was so distressed that he had an attack almost immediately. But not before he wrote me the letter…'

Julia was very pale now. 'Lewis, I protest—'

'As you wish,' Lewis said inexorably. 'I know from Churchward that the Admiral vouchsafed con-siderable sums to you over the years and that your own fortune was finished years ago. Jack Chessford was a gambler, was he not? And I believe you adopted the same expensive vice.'

He looked across at Richard Slater, who had kept silent during the whole exchange. 'There are plenty of people who have seen you run through a fortune in one sitting, Julia! And as always, you applied to my father to pay your debts. Only this time, he refused to help you!'

'This is monstrous!' Julia was looking wildly from Caroline to Richard Slater. 'They are all out to discredit me! Your so-called friends and my companion…' She burst into noisy sobs. 'It is iniquitous!'

Lewis was looking grave. 'So reluctant was Richard to tell me what he knew that I had to confide all my own suspicions first! As for Miss Whiston, she scarcely deserves your censure—'

Julia sniffed furiously. 'Oh, do not speak of her! Treacherous creature!'

'She has spoken not one word against you,' Lewis said, gently, smiling at Caroline. 'But let me finish. You had a quarrel with my father, a bad one. When you realised that he did not intend to give you the money, you threatened to spread slanderous gossip. You told him that you would say he had tried to force you to marry my brother, that he had then pressed his own suit, that he was a satyr who had abused his own position as your guardian to maltreat you! None of it was true, but it would make a good story! My father reacted furiously and you stormed out, intending to leave immediately. Then, you heard that he had been struck down by the attack that would eventually kill him.'

Lewis turned away. His voice was toneless. 'You decided to stay at Hewly. It was a convenient place to hide from your creditors, you knew you might inherit something if my father died, and Lavender told you that I was returning home. There were all sorts of possibilities.' He sighed. 'It was not for a while that you heard the rumour that my father had been writing something when he was taken ill, but then the horrid thought took you that perhaps it had been an alteration to his will, made with the intention of cutting you out altogether!'

Lewis looked across at Letty, who was sitting quietly, head bent. 'Unbeknownst to you, it was your own opportunistic maid who had hidden the letter, intending to come back for it later and make use of it as best she could! She was planning a little blackmail of her own, but you made it worth her while to join forces with you! Unfortunately, however, she had forgotten quite where she had hidden it, and the two of you were obliged to sift through every book in the whole house, and then without success!'

He crossed to the table, took out the letter and placed it down by Julia's side. 'Here it is. *You* were the ghostly figure who was wandering about the house after my father died, but you were on a more earthly quest! You did not wish to lose what little money had been left to you!'

Caroline found her voice. 'But if the letter does not

contain an alteration to your father's will, Captain Brabant, what does it say?'

There was grim humour in Lewis's voice. 'I doubt that my father would have had time to make a legal amendment to his will even had he wished to. But that was not his aim. Angry, outraged by Julia's threats, he cared more about honour than money. My father was at pains to tell me that your accusations were untrue, Julia, and that if you should ever seek to besmirch his memory, you would be telling falsehoods. He told me that you petitioned to marry Andrew of your own free will—both Lavender and Mrs Prior bear this out. You ran away with Jack Chessford because you were bored and Jack had a fortune—before he gamed it all away, of course! So—' Lewis finished quietly '—your lies are ended. Not even the theft of Miss Whiston's letters was enough to save you!'

Caroline looked startled, but Letty, whose nerves were clearly in shreds, started to sob again. 'I'm sorry, miss! I burned every one of them like she told me!'

Caroline shook her head in bewilderment. 'Never mind, Letty. I doubt it matters after all else that has happened.'

'My father had already been disillusioned by you when Andrew died, Julia,' Lewis finished quietly. 'He added the bizarre stipulation to his will to try to dissuade me from ever marrying you. He need not have troubled himself. I have seldom heard such an ugly tale of double-dealing and deceit, and I was already suspicious of it before I ever had his letter.'

Julia leaped to her feet. Her eyes were wild and two bright spots of colour burned feverishly in her cheeks. 'That being so, Captain Brabant, I shall remove from your house at once!'

'You shall!' Lewis seemed amused rather than anything else. 'I am obliged to you!'

'But do not seek to try to cut me out of the will!' Julia added viciously, as she headed for the door. 'I am entitled to that money for tolerating Uncle Harley's tedious company for all those years! And as for you—' she turned on Caroline with a fury that made her flinch back '—with your scheming ways, I wish you happy! I can do much better for myself than a miserable sea captain with no title and a tiny fortune!'

'Which is probably true,' Lewis said cheerfully, as the slam of the library door echoed through the whole house. His eye fell on the maid, who was shrinking in her chair. 'Well, run along, girl,' he said, not unkindly. 'Your mistress will need help with her packing! The two of you deserve each other!'

Caroline sat down rather heavily in the chair that Julia had vacated. There was a silence. 'A glass of wine, perhaps,' Richard Slater said, moving across to the sideboard. 'I believe we are all in need of fortification!'

'She took so many risks!' Caroline said, still thinking of Julia and the enormity of what she had done.

'She's a gambler,' Lewis said shortly. 'Reckless risk has become part of her life. Perhaps it always was…'

Caroline gratefully accepted a glass from Richard and drank deeply, welcoming the reviving warmth. She shivered. 'This is a nasty business, Captain Slater. How did you know that Julia was so deep in debt?'

Richard Slater looked uncomfortable. 'It was gossip only, which was why I was at pains not to pass it on to Lewis. My sister Fanny had been in London the Season past, and commented to me that Mrs Chessford was playing deep and on the watch for a rich husband. I believe she only mentioned it because she knew of Mrs Chessford's connection with Lewis's family…' He shrugged. 'I thought little of it until Lewis told me of the Admiral's letter.'

'Speaking of letters,' Caroline turned her enquiring gaze upon Lewis, 'how did you know that it was Julia who had taken mine?'

Lewis stretched. He gave her a mischievous grin. 'My dear Caroline, when you accused me of stealing your property you had forgotten one important fact! You thought that I was the only one who had known of the existence of the letters, but there were always two—myself and Julia. After all, she had written them and knew what they contained! When I told her of the incident of the letter left in *Marmion*, she immediately realised how incriminating they would be and how they contradicted her own story! So,' he shrugged, 'she took them, or had Letty steal them for her.'

Caroline thought of the artless phrases the young Julia had written when she was planning to throw Lewis over in favour of Andrew Brabant. There was no doubt that they conflicted dramatically with the tale that she had been forced unwillingly into the betrothal and they would have done her much harm had they come to light.

Lewis shifted slightly. 'I have to confess that I read more of that letter than I first admitted, Miss Whiston! It was that that planted the first doubts in my mind when Julia tried to pretend she had not wished to marry Andrew.' He cleared his throat and quoted dryly: '"Of course, Andrew is the elder and so will inherit the Admiral's fortune one day, which is so much more comfortable than having to scratch around on a sailor's income…"'

'Oh dear…' Caroline said, grimacing.

'Well, I have to agree with her,' Richard Slater said with a grin. 'A most practical woman, Mrs Chessford!' He yawned. 'Excuse me, I am worn to a thread with all this Cheltenham tragedy! I will see you both in the morning!'

He drained his glass and sauntered out of the room. Left alone with Lewis, Caroline felt suddenly and unaccountably shy. She avoided his eyes.

'I think I should retire also, sir. It is very late—'

'And you seem to have a penchant for creeping about the house in your night attire,' Lewis observed, his gaze wandering over her in a thoroughly disconcerting manner. 'Miss Whiston, there is something I wish to ask you. It has nothing to do with what has just passed, and no doubt it should wait until the morning, but I find I cannot wait.'

He got to his feet and pulled her up too. Caroline's gaze searched his face, a little bewildered. 'Sir?'

'Miss Whiston.' Lewis kept hold of her hand, grown suddenly cold, in his. 'You must be aware of the regard I have for you. I should therefore deem it an honour if you would consent to be my wife.'

Caroline was not sure how long it was that she stared up into his face. 'You are precipitate, Captain Brabant,' she managed to say, after a pause. 'You have only just cleared your decks—'

'And having done so, I believe in aiming for my goal. It was what I had intended all along. Perhaps I should have waited, but as I said, I could not.'

Lewis was watching her face intently. Caroline looked away, unwilling to give her own feelings away.

'I am honoured by your regard, sir,' she said uncertainly, 'but I must have time to think. After all, I was obliged to hear rather more than I wished this evening of your affections for another lady!'

Lewis's tense expression lightened a little. 'Affection be damned!' He gave her hands a little shake. 'Surely you must see that I cannot bear Julia? Oh, I admit that for a while I was at her feet—impressionable youths must be allowed to make mistakes in their salad days! But she was always a mercenary piece! Even when I went away to sea she asked for a keepsake and took me to task for presenting her with a necklace of pearls rather than one of diamonds!'

Caroline tried unsuccessfully to smother a giggle.

'Alas that your judgement of women is so faulty, Captain!'

'Not this time,' Lewis said.

'And then there is the question of your more recent behaviour,' Caroline pursued. 'You were seen embracing Mrs Chessford, and yet you denied it!'

Lewis raised his eyebrows. 'My dear Caroline, you have already accused me of this once! If you refer to the occasion when Julia cast herself into my arms in floods of tears, then I suppose I must plead guilty! There was nothing in it but if Lavender saw—' He shrugged. 'I suppose she may not know the difference!'

He slanted a look down at her. 'Perhaps you might make the same mistake? Allow me to demonstrate…'

He smiled down at her for a moment, then bent his head and kissed her gently. Caroline resisted briefly, but the temptation was too delicious to withstand. Her lips parted and he deepened the kiss immediately, tasting, teasing, until compelling pleasure sent her mind reeling. She was dimly aware of Lewis pulling her closer, and she slid her arms about his neck, all thoughts lost in the delight of sensation. One could drown in such pleasure…

'Your answer, Caro…' Lewis's words were barely above a whisper. 'Say you will marry me…'

His mouth had left hers and was brushing the sensitive skin just below her left ear, sending shivers of excitement coursing through Caroline's blood. His mouth drifted lower to the hollow at the base of her throat, then down to the soft swell of skin above the lace of her nightgown. Caroline caught her breath.

'Lewis, wait…' She stepped back and tried to extricate herself. 'I must think…'

'Must you?' Lewis loosened his grip a little but did not let her go. 'Just for once, Caro, could you not put aside your customary cool detachment? The romantic Miss Whiston I met in the woods had no such scruples…'

Caroline laughed a little shakily. Cool detachment was hardly the way to describe her feelings. 'I think you took advantage of me then, sir—'

'A delightful thought! But, no—' He had felt her instinctive movement of protest and let her go '—the time and place are scarcely right. I know I should have waited to ask you. I will give you until tomorrow for an answer, but Caro—' she looked up at his tone and met the determination in his eyes '—do not think to refuse me.' He pulled her back to him and gave her a brief, hard kiss that held a disturbing echo of their former passion. 'Now I had better let you go.'

The morning had come. Caroline lay in bed and watched the shadows move on her ceiling, the curious white light that suggested that there was thick snow outside. She had slept late after the events of the previous night, falling into a deep, dreamless sleep as soon as she had tumbled into bed. There had been no time to reflect on either the extraordinary revelations about Julia or the more pressing problem of Lewis's proposal.

Just why was it a problem? Caroline turned on her side and heaved a sigh. She cared deeply for Lewis and had done so almost from the first moment she had met him. She believed him when he said that he no longer cared a rush for Julia, so it was not as though she felt she was living in a shadow of another woman. Their mutual passion was as intriguing as it was explosive, but perhaps she should not think of that, for it was enough to blind her to all else…

Caroline shifted uncomfortably. She had lived her whole adult life without succumbing to physical desire and it was only now that she realised how vulnerable this had made her, affecting her judgement, making her uncertain… For the nub of the problem was that Lewis might no longer love Julia, but that did not necessarily mean that he loved her.

Caroline faced the thought plainly and sadly. Lewis had to marry to fulfil the terms of his father's will. Who better than the convenient companion, a woman with no expectations, sensible, plain, a good manager who would help him turn the estate around? Put in such straightforward terms and shorn of the misleading confusion of physical attraction, it seemed a little bleak.

That did not mean, of course, that she had to refuse him. Caroline got out of bed, washed and started to dress, all the time preoccupied with her thoughts. It was an opportunity that any governess companion would give their eye teeth for. She had only to say yes.

She stared into the mirror, wondering why the

thought gave her such difficulty. Her wan face looked back at her. The reason was not far to seek. She had fallen in love with Lewis Brabant and wanted him to love her too. Anything less was not enough; physical passion, companionship, a home… Caroline shook her head. How foolish, when she had had none of these things a few months ago, and now had been offered the world! Almost all the world. Yet somehow, without Lewis's love, it was not enough.

Caroline was not surprised to find that Julia was not at the breakfast table. Lavender was present and had evidently received a foreshortened explanation of the events of the previous night from her brother, for she was looking shocked and pale. Lewis had finished eating and had progressed to his newspaper; Richard Slater was placidly demolishing a plate of devilled kidneys. It seemed to Caroline that everyone was trying a little too hard to behave as though nothing had happened.

Caroline sat down and returned their greetings a little self-consciously. She was very aware of Lewis's gaze resting upon her, of a contained restlessness about him that was even more noticeable than previously. Caroline could hardly pretend that she did not know its cause and her nerves tightened in anticipation of the interview to come. She accepted a plate of toast, then promptly found that her appetite had deserted her.

Lewis put down his newspaper and got to his feet. 'Miss Whiston, would you grant me the pleasure of your company as soon as it is convenient? In the study. Preferably now.'

Caroline hesitated. Richard continued to eat his breakfast whilst Lavender looked speculatively from one to the other. Caroline capitulated.

It was with some trepidation that she preceded Lewis into the familiar room and waited whilst he closed the door. She pressed her hands together to give herself courage.

'Well?' Lewis spoke softly. He had come to her and taken her hand, and his touch almost undid all her resolutions. Caroline moved away.

'Captain Brabant, I am conscious of the honour you do me but…' She met his eyes and looked quickly away. 'I fear I must decline your offer.'

Lewis was very still for a moment. 'I see. Will you do me the courtesy of explaining why you reject my suit?'

Caroline bit her lip. This was dreadful, worse by far than disappointing poor Mr Grizel, for in refusing Lewis she was going against her own feelings as well as rejecting him. She wrung her hands.

'You seem in some distress, Miss Whiston,' Lewis said quietly. 'Pray tell me what I may do to help you.'

Caroline cast him an agonised glance. 'There is nothing you can do, sir, save not to press me for a reason—'

Lewis gave her an ironic smile. 'Then it seems I must be cruel, for I do most ardently wish to know your reasons, Miss Whiston.'

Caroline's feelings got the better of her like a dam

bursting. She abandoned polite restraint. 'There are one hundred and one reasons why we should not wed, Captain, as you are well aware! The most obvious one is that the dispositions of your father's will mean you are obliged to marry! You can scarcely expect me to feel flattered, the convenient bride!'

'The devil!' Lewis seemed genuinely amused, which only served to irritate Caroline the more. 'My dear Caroline, please do not suggest that I have proposed to you because I am lazy and you are convenient! Such assumptions do credit to neither of us!'

'It is what everyone will think—'

'Who cares a rush about that? *I* do not think it, and now that I have told you there is no truth in the accusation, you may disregard it too!'

'Leaving that aside, sir,' Caroline said hastily, 'there are other considerations! I am—was—Mrs Chessford's companion, and it would be most—'

'I hope you are not going to say that it would be inappropriate!' For a moment, Lewis looked dangerous. 'Caroline, you are a Whiston of Watchbell Hall, if you insist on social distinctions, and even if you were not from a good family, I would not care tuppence! You will have to do better than that!'

'There will be a lot of talk,' Caroline said desperately.

Lewis shrugged indifferently. 'There always is! Let them talk!'

'And then,' Caroline said, grasping at straws, 'there is my age, sir.'

'Your age!' Lewis looked completely incredulous.

'I believe that you should marry someone younger, someone more...' Caroline broke off in slight confusion.

Lewis looked as though he were not sure whether to laugh or lose his temper. 'Caroline, that reason is contemptible! You are scarce in your dotage! Besides, I should run mad if I were married to some brainless débutante!'

'There are some very sensible young girls,' Caroline began, but Lewis stopped her with a gesture. 'Please, Caroline, do not insult my intelligence with any more of your spurious excuses! It is clear to me that there are other reasons, ones that you do not see fit to disclose. Well, I have a solution.'

He reached her side in only two strides. 'The correct course of action is not an appeal through the intellect at this stage. Caroline—' his arms slid about her waist '—I know that you are not indifferent to me, and I, for my part, find you most deliciously attractive! You may have as much time to think as you wish, but please succumb to your romantic side and accept my proposal!'

Caroline gave a despairing squeak. She could feel herself weakening, both literally and metaphorically. Lewis tightened his grip and bent to kiss her. Caroline felt her lips tremble beneath his. Then, to her huge disappointment, he let her go and stepped back.

'You will not accept me and I will not accept your refusal,' he said evenly. 'So, Miss Whiston, until we may come to some agreement, that is the way it will stay!'

Chapter Eleven

'So Julia has gone,' Lavender said contentedly, biting heartily into a slice of Cook's sponge cake. 'Did you hear the fuss she made, Caroline? Still, I cannot envy her having to travel in this weather!'

The snow was no longer falling but it lay thick on the ground in drifts of up to two foot deep.

'I suppose she may not make London by nightfall,' Lavender continued, not sounding much concerned, 'and will have to put up somewhere on the road. Ah well, the house is the more peaceful for it!'

This was odd but true. Caroline had already noticed that a certain tension seemed to have gone from the atmosphere. The servants were smiling more. The cuckoo had gone from the nest.

'You are very quiet,' Lavender said suddenly, fixing Caroline with the perceptive blue gaze that was so like her brother's. 'Is something troubling you, Caroline? It is unlike you to be so silent whilst I chatter on!'

Caroline shook her head. 'No, not precisely. That

is…' She gave Lavender an anxious look. 'I feel a little awkward now that Julia has gone and I am still here! I must make plans…'

'Well, there is no hurry!' Lavender said, gesturing with the cake in her hand. She put it down hastily as a few crumbs scattered on the carpet. 'How unladylike of me! I suppose I am too old for your teaching, Caroline? You could always stay as my governess rather than my companion!'

Caroline smiled and frowned at the same time. 'Now Lavender, we have had this conversation!'

'I know it!' The younger girl sighed. 'I do not understand why I cannot persuade you! Oh, that reminds me…' She fumbled in her pocket. 'I have a letter here for you! I almost forgot! Perhaps it will be the good news you are awaiting.'

Caroline took the letter with some trepidation. The writing was that of Lady Covingham, and suddenly Caroline was uncertain whether she wished to stay or to go. Impatient with herself, she tore it open.

'Is something wrong?' Lavender asked, a moment later, her gaze resting on Caroline's face. 'You look a little disappointed, Caroline…'

'Yes, no… I don't know,' Caroline pulled herself together and gave Lavender a weak smile. 'Lady Covingham writes that the family she had had in mind for me have already appointed a governess and so will not be needing my services. She says that she will continue to search for a position for me, but…' Caroline's voice trailed away. 'Oh, never mind! I shall just have to change my plans.'

'Capital!' Lavender said, clapping her hands and ignoring Caroline's frown of disapproval at her language. 'You may stay here for a spell instead! That will give Lewis the chance—' She stopped and clapped her hand to her mouth. 'Oh dear...' She looked quickly at Caroline's face. 'Well, it was an open secret...'

'Was it indeed!' Caroline said wrathfully. 'Your brother has not spoken to you of it?'

'Of course not!' Lavender looked indignant. 'He would not! But anyone with any sense can see that Lewis cares for you, Caroline!' She gave a pleasurable little shiver. 'Sometimes when he looks at you—'

Caroline raised her eyebrows and decided that this was not the moment to try to explain the difference between physical attraction and love. Lavender's face was suddenly wistful. 'I wish...' She broke off. 'Oh, I know it is none of my business, Caroline, but if you have refused Lewis because you think he is only interested in marrying to fulfil the will, you are fair and far out! Why, it is plain to me that he loves you and I know you care for him too!'

Caroline smiled a little sadly. 'That is not all, though, is it, Lavender? Only think how people will talk! The Captain and the companion—'

'Let them!' Lavender said robustly. 'Anyway, you are wrong if you think that the neighbourhood would not approve! Why, only last week Lady Perceval said to me that you were a charming girl, just like your mama, and that she hoped that you would find you would be spending longer at Hewly than you had first thought!'

Caroline raised her eyebrows at this sign of approbation. 'Well…'

'Think about it!' Lavender said, patting her hand and suddenly sounding far older than her years. 'I am persuaded that you will find that most of your objections do not truly exist!'

'Perhaps you are right,' Caroline said, getting up. 'I shall go for a walk and give the matter some thought! It is time I cleared my head!'

'Only do not stray too far!' Lavender called after her. 'Belton says that it will snow again later!'

The gardens were completely transformed under their blanket of white. Heavy branches bowed down under the weight of snow and the sun was blinding. The snow crunched under Caroline's boots as she walked. She was wearing a thick winter cloak, a warm scarf, gloves—and the red velvet dress, for if she was to make the most momentous decision of her life she wished to do it in style.

The sunlight glittered on the icy surface of the Steep river and Caroline walked on, deep in thought. Lavender was probably correct and all her objections were insubstantial ones. She would make a good mistress of Hewly, she loved Lewis deeply and if he truly loved her… Well, there was only one way to find that out. She would have to ask him. Caroline squared her shoulders. It was a daunting thought but she would prepare carefully and approach him in a sensible and rational manner. Then, if the answer was not as she hoped, she would be able to withdraw with what dignity she had left and consider an alternative plan...

An icicle dripped from the tree above her head. Caroline jumped and looked around her. She was disconcerted to realise that she had wandered quite far into the forest whilst she had been thinking. The blue shadows were gathering beneath the silent trees and it was almost dusk. She looked around for the path, but nothing was visible beneath the white covering of snow. Her own footsteps stretched behind her as far as she could see. Turning around, Caroline hurried back the way she had come.

Within a half hour she was no nearer the edge of the forest and she was forced to concede that she was lost. Darkness was falling and it had started to snow again, just as Belton had predicted, obliterating her footprints and making it even more unlikely that she would find her way back. Caroline was very angry with herself. Of all the foolish starts, to go wandering off in the snow without so much as a second thought of how she might find her way! Everything was now covered by a fresh layer of snow and she was completely disorientated. Nor were there any lights to guide her. Caroline fought down a wave of panic and continued to pick her way through the trees, taking care not to stumble over a hidden root. It was slow going in the snow, and she was feeling both hungry and tired now. The hem of the cloak and the were both soaking, and Caroline's feet with cold.

She had almost given up hope of shelter when she stumbled across the hut. It was more substantial than the one in which she had hidden on the day she had first met Lewis, for the roof and all the walls were sound. Indeed, when Caroline stumbled inside she found it to be furnished in a rough fashion, although deserted. There was a stump of a candle in a dish and dry brushwood in the fireplace, a pitcher of water and a long truckle bed against the wall, as well as a few other sticks of furniture.

Caroline closed the door against the snowy night and groped her way across to the table. After four attempts she managed to strike the tinder and light the candle, which proved to be tallow and smelled strongly. Caroline did not care. She lit the brushwood fire, stoked it to a blaze and stripped off her cloak and soaking dress. Then, huddled before the fire in her shift, she wrapped the cloak around her once more and tried to get warm.

It seemed that the hut was the base for woodcutters or possibly those engaged in more furtive work. Caroline thought it unlikely in the extreme than any poachers would be out that night, so she counted on having the place to herself. That said, it was draughty, uncomfortable and cold, but it was shelter and she would have to stay in it until the daylight brought either rescue or at least the chance of finding her way back to the path. Caroline thought guiltily of Lavender, who had warned her not to walk too far and would now be beside herself with worry. Lewis would probably be furious… But there was nothing

to be done. At last she was starting to feel warm and
the warmth made her drowsy. She banked the fire
down, lay down on the rough bed and drew the cloak
about her as best she could. She blew out the candle
and almost immediately fell asleep.

Caroline had no idea how long it was before she
awoke. It was still dark, and from outside the hut
came the scrape of metal on stone. She sat bolt upright, suddenly terrified. If this was a poachers' hide-
out and she was here, alone in just her shift in the
middle of the night... Even as the thoughts rushed
through her mind, there was a crash and the door was
flung open. In the aperture stood Lewis Brabant and
he looked furiously angry. He held a carriage lamp
high in one hand, the candle inside shedding its light
over the interior of the hut and shining into Caroline's
eyes. Behind him, the darkness swirled with flakes of
white. Lewis came into the hut and closed the door
behind him, shaking the snow from his cloak.
Caroline found her voice.

'Lewis! Oh, thank God, it's you! I had quite given
up hope!'

Her words did not appear to have a soothing effect,
for Lewis still looked furious. 'Had you indeed, madam? Yet you seem quite comfortable here whilst the
rest of us tramp through the snow searching for you!'

His gaze swept over her, taking in the warm firelight, the makeshift bed and Caroline, her hair dried
in curls about her shoulders. An indefinable look
came into his eyes, one that made Caroline suddenly
self-conscious. She started to rise, remembered that

she was in her shift, and pulled the cloak more securely about her.

'I was making do until help arrived,' she said hastily, 'but now that you are here, Lewis, we may return to the house—'

Lewis gave her a scorching look. He removed his cloak and arranged it beside Caroline's dress in front of the fire, kicking the glowing embers into life again.

'Return to the house? You must be mad if you think that I would step outside again in that weather!' He came across to the bed and sat down on the edge, grasping Caroline by the shoulders. 'I have sent the others back and I was about to give up and go home myself! Have you any idea what I have been through, Caroline, searching for you from barn to byre, calling your name, looking for footprints until I thought all hope was lost!' He shook her. 'And now that I am here I will not stir again until the snow has ceased and neither will you!'

The cloak had slipped. Caroline folded her arms firmly across her breasts.

'But we cannot stay here—' she began, only to be silenced by the infuriated glare Lewis gave her. She started to realise that he was even more angry than she had first thought.

'Pray do not argue with me, madam!' His tone was as arctic as the weather. 'I suppose you will tell me next that it is inappropriate for us to be alone! All I can say is that you should have thought of that before wandering off and putting us all to an unconscionable amount of trouble!' The fury took hold of him again.

'Good God, you of all people should know that there are poachers in these woods—'

'Well, they will not be out tonight!' Caroline retorted, as angry as him now.

'No!' Lewis stood up and turned away to put more wood on the fire. 'They will not! No one else would be so stupid! Of all the addle-pated little fools! What were you doing—running away from me? If my proposal was so unwelcome you need only have said! I would not have pressed my suit further!'

Caroline frowned. 'Of course I was not running away! How can you be so nonsensical! I went for a walk and wandered from the path by the veriest accident!'

'Hm,' Lewis looked slightly mollified. He straightened up. The fire was burning brightly now, filling the hut with light and warmth and shadows. Caroline snuggled back under her cloak.

'By all means make yourself comfortable by the fire!' she said sleepily. 'If we are indeed to stay here until daylight you must try to rest...'

'Thank you!' Lewis sat down on the edge of the bed and pulled his boots off, sending them crashing across the hut, where they bounced against the door. 'I confess that sleep is not the matter on my mind at the moment.'

Caroline, whose eyes had just started to close, opened them again hastily. She was in time to see him discard his jacket and pull his shirt over his head. She drew back with a gasp of alarm.

'Lewis, I only meant—'

'Yes?' He turned on her suddenly. 'Just what did you mean, Caroline? I believe you gave me your word that you would not stray from Hewly again, yet I find you foolishly walking in the snow, wandering from the path…'

Caroline, totally intimidated by the presence of a semi-naked man so close to her, shrank back against the wall of the hut. 'I was only… I wished to have some time to think… I took my book of poetry…'

Lewis' gaze travelled over her slowly, taking in her flushed face and stormy hazel eyes. He deliberately dropped his gaze to her bare shoulders and the cloak that Caroline was now desperately clutching beneath her chin. Caroline felt the heat come up to her skin, suddenly suffusing her from head to toe. Lewis looked from her to the red velvet dress, draped across the wooden chair before the fire. He started to smile, but it did not reassure Caroline at all, edged as it was with predatory intent.

'Well, well,' Lewis said cordially, 'so you decided to go for a walk… In your evening dress, in the snow… And to think that I have been waiting this age for your romantic inclinations to triumph and when they do they almost kill us both! Yet I find that I am glad, after all…'

Caroline found that there was nowhere further to retreat to, for her back was against the wall and she was becoming decidedly chilly. She tried to wriggle under the cloak, but Lewis was too quick for her. He across her and pulled her beneath him in one swift move, trapping her with his weight. Caroline squirmed.

'Lewis, what—'

Her words were cut off as his mouth came down fiercely, violently, plundering the softness of hers. A delicious warmth flooded through her, a trembling and tingling that left her utterly confused. His lips were parting her own ruthlessly, his tongue sliding between them with a merciless demand that left her reeling. Caroline gasped and he took immediate advantage to deepen the kiss, sending her senses spinning. His hands tangled in her hair; his mouth moved over hers in total supremacy.

Caroline came to her senses briefly when Lewis let her go for a moment and she realised that he was removing the last of his clothes. The firelight slid across his hard, muscular body in slabs of red and shadow and Caroline lay still and watched, unable to tear her gaze away.

'Lewis,' her words came out as a whisper, 'is this really necessary…?'

His shadow seemed to stoop like a hawk as he leaned across her, taking her lips in another insistent kiss.

'Yes, my darling Caro, it is entirely necessary.' His voice was very husky. 'But before we go any further there is something I should tell you. The church is booked for Saturday morning—two days' time, or indeed it might only be one day by now, and I shall brook no opposition. I have a special licence. And if you still think that I do not love you…'

Caroline's eyes flew wide. 'You love me? I did not realise—'

'Are you quite mad?' For a moment Lewis looked fierce again. 'How much more obvious does it need to be…?'

Caroline could not answer as he kissed her for a third time. His skin was warm beneath her fingers, intriguingly taut and soft at the same time… She smoothed her hand across his chest experimentally and heard him groan as he slid down beside her on the truckle bed.

'I thought that you were married to your ship,' she said at last, a hint of teasing in the words as she looked up into the blue eyes so close to hers. 'I am sure that you said that she was brave and true…'

'So she was, and I swore not to marry until I found a woman to match her…'

Lewis stripped back the covering cloak and his fingers found the laces of Caroline's shift. She caught her breath as he dealt efficiently with the bows and brushed the material aside impatiently.

'I protest— You have done this before, Lewis…'

He laughed. 'What, do you think I am a rake, then? Prim Miss Whiston will have no truck with rakes…'

He bent his head to her breast and Caroline cried out at once, arching against him. This was a whole new world of sensation, urgent, melting…

'Severe Miss Whiston…' Lewis's voice was rough now as his hands moved softly over her exposed skin '…would never indulge in such inappropriate behaviour as this…' He slid the shift down over her hips. 'I am persuaded that she would be quite horrified at such unsuitable conduct…' He trailed tiny kisses down her throat and over her breasts until Caroline was almost crying with need.

'Do you know how much I have longed to find my own sweet Caro again?' Lewis said softly. 'I knew that she was only hiding and now that I have found her I will never let her go…'

'Lewis,' Caroline could barely concentrate, but she had something to tell him. 'Did I tell you that I love you too…'

She saw the blaze of triumph in his eyes. 'Darling Caro…'

Caroline reached out and slid her hands over his back, gasping with pleasure at the feel of him beneath her fingers, pulling him closer. Every inch of her was burning for him and when Lewis brought his mouth back down to hers she writhed with delight and drew him to her, aware of nothing but the spiralling desire that threatened to consume her.

'Please, Lewis—'

'Oh, Miss Whiston—' his eyes were mocking her but there was a heat there that matched her own '—pleasure should not be hurried!'

'Later,' Caroline whispered, arching against him, 'later you may take your time…'

She heard him laugh and it was the last conscious thing that she remembered in the whirl of sensation that engulfed her. She had no thought for convention or appropriate behaviour. Prim Miss Whiston was gone for ever.

It was cold in the hut and Caroline burrowed deeper under the covers, closer to the warm, male body entangled with hers. Lewis shifted slightly to accommodate her and drew her to him so that her cheek was resting in the curve of his shoulder.

'Lewis, you say that we are to be married in two days…'

'One day. It is past midnight.' His voice was a sleepy murmur.

'But I have not yet agreed to your proposal…' Caroline was tracing her fingers over his chest. She leant closer and saw the corner of his mouth lift in a smile.

'So you have not. Will you run away instead, then?'

'I might…'

'And I would have to bring you back and tell anyone who cares to challenge me that you are absconding with the family silver…'

Caroline wriggled closer, lowering her lips to within an inch of his. Drowsy blue eyes smiled into hers.

'Is there any?' she whispered.

'Mmm…' Lewis made an effort to stir himself. 'I am sure I could find some to substantiate my claims…'

He reached out a lazy hand and pulled her back down beside him. With one finger, he traced a line down the soft skin on the inside of her arm, pausing as his hand brushed the side of her breast. Caroline started to tremble.

'Do you think that you will like being married to me, Caro?'

'It will be tolerable,' Caroline gasped, as his hand drifted across her bare stomach. 'Of course, you will have to behave sensibly—'

'I have no intention of doing so, I assure you. Is this sensible?' Lewis bent over and kissed the corner of her mouth softly. 'Is this?' His hand cupped her breast, stroking gently.

'Lewis?'

'Yes, Caro?' The gentle movement did not cease.

Caroline shivered. 'It is not really appropriate to repeat your actions so soon—'

Lewis leant over her. 'Yet I distinctly remember you telling me that I might do so. Slowly, as well...'

Caroline abandoned the unequal attempt to think straight. There was no necessity for it. Probably, she thought blissfully, as Lewis started to kiss her again, very slowly, there would never be any need to be strict and prim and appropriate again.

'Caroline, brave and beautiful,' Lewis whispered against her skin. 'My dauntless Caro, the perfect companion. I believe that I have truly met my match!'

MILLS & BOON®

Makes any time special™

Mills & Boon publish 29 new titles every month. Select from...

Modern Romance™   Tender Romance™

Sensual Romance™

Medical Romance™   Historical Romance™

MAT2

A Perfect Family

An enthralling family saga by bestselling author

PENNY JORDAN

Published 20th July